MARINE PROTECTOR

BROTHERHOOD PROTECTORS WORLD

DEBRA PARMLEY

Copyright © 2018, Debra Parmley

Cover art by Sheri L. McGathy

This book is a work of fiction. Names, characters, places and incidents are products of the author's imagination or used fictitiously. Any resemblance to actual events, locales or persons living or dead is entirely coincidental.

© 2018 Twisted Page Press, LLC ALL RIGHTS RESERVED

No part of this book may be used, stored, reproduced or transmitted without written permission from the publisher except for brief quotations for review purposes as permitted by law.

This book is licensed for your personal enjoyment only. This book may not be re-sold or given away to other people. If you would like to share this book with another person, please purchase an additional copy for each recipient. If you're reading this book and did not purchase it, or it was not purchased for your use only, please purchase your own copy.

BROTHERHOOD PROTECTORS

ORIGINAL SERIES BY ELLE JAMES

Brotherhood Protectors Series
Montana SEAL (#1)
Bride Protector SEAL (#2)
Montana D-Force (#3)
Cowboy D-Force (#4)
Montana Ranger (#5)
Montana Dog Soldier (#6)
Montana SEAL Daddy (#7)
Montana Ranger's Wedding Vow (#8)
Montana SEAL Undercover Daddy (#9)
Cape Cod SEAL Rescue (#10)
Montana SEAL Friendly Fire (#11)
Montana SEAL's Bride (#12)
Montana Rescue
Hot SEAL, Salty Dog

To the men and women of the USMC, who protect and defend our constitution and our country.

ACKNOWLEDGMENTS

Thank you to Elle James for opening Twisted Pages Press LLC, for your love and support, and for your patience with this book and me. Thank you to Delilah Devlin, my editor, who jumped in at the last minute, making it possible for me to finish this book. Thank you to my cover artist, Sheri L. McGathy, for the beautiful cover.

To my husband Mike, thank you for handling things so I can write, and for many years of love and support. Thank you to my sister and PA, Kimberly Lear, for love and support, and all the things too numerous to list here.

Thank you to Francesca Anastasi aka Sabeya,

founder of the annual, international event Shimmy Mob. I'm blessed and honored to have been a small part of your fundraising work. Thank you to all who helped with Shimmy Mob Memphis, and who continue to support our local domestic abuse shelters.

CHAPTER 1

I WILL BE free of Z.

She thought the mantra again. It was what kept her going when things weren't going. When it seemed like she'd never be free from him.

RED JUMPED, staring out the window of the bus headed to Eagle Rock, Montana as five Harleys roared by, startling her. She slid down in her seat and leaned her head away from the glass, forgetting about the blonde wig she wore as a disguise.

"Noisy, ain't they?" The gray-haired man sitting in the seat next to her asked.

"Yeah," she said.

He had no idea. Try riding on the back of one while surrounded by others roaring down the highway.

"Made me jump, too," The old guy said. "They cain't hurt you though. You're safe in here."

Great. Now this old guy will remember me as the woman who's afraid of motorcycles. We aren't supposed to give anyone anything to remember us by. And he's wrong about being safe. If Z found me here, he'd drag me out by my hair.

She sat up and looked out her window again. Montana, with its clear skies and wide-open spaces, was a perfect place to ride, especially on a sunny day like today. But the motorcycles, though hot and sexy as Harleys always are, no longer held appeal for her. She'd vowed, from now on, to stay away from Harleys and the men who rode them.

She wasn't a big joiner, not any more. Joining things was dangerous. Any group you joined had people who expected something from you. But the Triple C Ranch in Eagle Rock, Montana, was the place for her new start, and while there, she'd have to join in and be part of the group. That was part of the deal she'd made with the counselor.

She'd do the group stuff she had to do but otherwise wanted to be left alone.

The Triple C, short for Courage and Confidence Center, was the newest retreat center for women who've escaped domestic abuse situations or other attacks. The plan was the women would come to the ranch and gain new self-confidence, along with skills to help them in their new lives when they relocated.

A limo would pick up Red at her final bus station and take her to the ranch. The limo service donated rides for all who went to the center, forming another layer of protection. If followed, the limo would go in another direction, not the ranch.

The head of the shelter in Chicago had suggested the center to her, and she was lucky to be going. Not every woman got in. There was a waiting list and a bunch of hoops to jump through to even be put on that list.

First, she'd had to meet each goal. A doctor had to certify she was drug and alcohol free, as well as fit to travel, swim, ride horses, and take a self-defense class. There could be no upcoming court appearances, and her finances had to be in order. Once at the center, she had to stay until she finished the program. If she had to leave for any reason, she couldn't go back. There was a sliding-fee scale based on income, and women were expected to contribute. Breaking a dependent cycle was part of the center's work with women who'd been attacked or abused—the goal, an independent, self-sufficient woman graduated and walked out that door.

Red made enough money to get in and to pay for her planned metamorphosis. She could always pick up another bartending or waitressing job, making it easier to move anywhere. She wasn't worried about that.

What she was worried about was someone on a motorcycle, like the Harleys that had roared past, recognizing her. Today, she wore a long-sleeved white blouse and ankle-length white skirt. The last thing she'd have worn anywhere, so it was the best way for her to hide. She was well hidden now, but she couldn't help her reaction to the bikes.

One of her three tattoos got under her skin in bad ways. She'd developed a habit of scratching at it, as if she could tear if off with her nails. The skin was nearly always red because she couldn't leave it alone. Now, it itched beneath her clothing, and she regretted pacing and digging at it the night before she'd left.

Nerves always made her need to move; she couldn't sit still when she was nervous.

She'd be changing clothes before getting into the

limo that was scheduled to pick her up at her last bus stop. Maybe if she put lotion on the scratches then, it would ease the itching. Then she'd waltz into that limo just like one of those celebrities who visited Montana.

Damn, skippy, I'm gonna enjoy that. Might as well make the most of it. Of everything. Life was too damn short not to live.

Out on the ranch, she was going to live free again. No more staying inside, behind high walls and closed curtains, hoping Z didn't find her.

Z-bear would kill her if he found her. He might drag her back into the gang first, but eventually he'd kill her. She wouldn't be the first person he'd killed. Z didn't like losing, and he'd lost respect in the gang by not keeping control of his woman.

Despite the tattoo on her skin that said "Property of Z", she belonged to no one but herself. He'd left his mark in visible and invisible places, but she was determined to erase every mark he'd made outside of her, inside of her, and anywhere else.

I will be free of Z.

She thought the mantra again. It was what kept her going when things weren't going.

She'd been eight months preparing and saving so

she could rise again, like a phoenix, after she left the ranch.

Sergeant Timothy, Tim "Timbers" Watson, formerly of the USMC, stood in the office of the Brotherhood Protectors meeting Hank Patterson in person. This was his first day on the job. He'd been restless after leaving the Marines and second-guessing his decision before the job offer to work for Hank came.

Even though he'd needed to be home for his dad, who'd been in the last stages of cancer, he'd been torn about leaving the corps and had longings to go back. After months back home, getting used to everyone calling him "Tim" again, he thought he'd adjusted to civilian life as well as he ever would. Still, something was missing.

Right after his dad passed, an invitation from the Brotherhood Protectors came in. Gunnery Sergeant Jack "Gunny" Barr, with whom he'd gone through basic training, had told Hank Patterson, the founder and owner, that Tim would be a good fit. Though not a Recon Marine like Gunny, Tim, as an infantry squad leader, had quickly made staff sergeant and was known to be an expert marksman.

When the call had come, he'd jumped at the offer. Now, he stood in Montana starting the first page in a new chapter in his life. He was ready for the adventure.

"Gunny speaks highly of you. Welcome to the Brotherhood Protectors," Hank said, shaking his hand.

"Thanks for allowing me to join you," Tim said.

"I've got an assignment for you, starting tomorrow. That gives you one day to settle in and to buy what you need. Pick out seven shirts from that closet," he said, pointing. "We'll have an I.D. ready for you today. The job is in L.A. You'll fly out tomorrow. Private plane. You'll be one in a four-man team. You already know Gunny, and you'll meet the others tomorrow."

Tim nodded. It would be good seeing Gunny again and working with him. Security for some rich celebrity would be a breeze compared to the desert of Iraq. Compared to caring for his dad those last weeks. A break from death was what he needed. Hank would keep him moving. He had no ties anywhere and told his new boss he'd go anywhere, any time he needed him.

Timbers became part of Hank's "away team", although he was based in Eagle Rock, with the others.

RED WAITED for her turn to get off the bus, deciding to get off last so as to be behind everyone. She preferred that to having people she didn't know behind her.

Trusting no one was the way to stay alive on this trip.

She'd managed to avoid saying more than a few words to anyone, by scowling at everyone. Blonde wig and white outfit aside, she wasn't going to let the wolves out there think she was a sweet naïve sheep, a tasty treat for some bad wolf. Like her favorite fairytale when she was a kid, she was aware there were big bad wolves in the world. She'd been in the hands of a very bad wolf. The problem was, she used to be attracted to him. And that had landed her where she was today. Now, she didn't want to be attracted to anybody.

She got off the bus and moved through the Montana heat rising up in the air, while staying aware of everyone around her as she made her way into the station and then the ladies' room.

She needed to be invisible. Just another woman passing through and forgotten.

Inside the stall, she peeled off the wig, the white blouse, and skirt. Wadding them up in a ball, she removed a black trash bag from her suitcase, and then stuffed everything into it. The white cotton outfit had at least been cool.

Montana in August is hot as hell. Hotter than anywhere I've ever been.

She fluffed out her short red hair and enjoyed the feel of air against her scalp. Her haircut was new. She'd had hair down her back when she was in the motorcycle club. This new short cut was supposed to be spikey on top but sweat from the wig had matted it to her head. She fluffed it again.

Taking a pair of jeans and a blue Mickey Mouse T-shirt from her suitcase, she changed, and then added socks and sneakers. Next, came the hat. A light grey ball cap with an embroidered horse on it, so the limo driver could identify her.

Putting her sunglasses on, she retrieved her suitcase and the trash bag, came out of the stall, and dropped the plastic bag into the trashcan.

Red moved toward the front door and the limo that was waiting at the curb.

That has to be the limo. The driver held a sign with the horse emblem.

She walked toward the limo in a normal gait, without her usual sass. Because that could give her away.

The driver opened the door for her, seeing her wearing the cap.

As she approached, he said, "Welcome to Montana. I hope you'll enjoy your stay and remember to wear sunscreen."

Sunscreen. The code word. Good. I'm safe.

"Thank you. Yes, I packed sunscreen, and I'm ready for sun." She answered in code, telling him she hadn't been followed.

As he held the door, she climbed in. He closed her door and put her suitcase in the trunk, and then went around to the driver's side to get in.

The limo driver looked into the mirror, and they made eye contact. "Phoebe Adams, nice to meet you. I'm Sam. Buckle up now and settle in."

"Call me Red." She hated the name Phoebe. Mostly because Z had called her Phoebes. Anything to put her down, once he thought she was completely his and the charming façade he'd worn at first had dropped. She'd be happy if she never heard that name again. Unfortunately, it was her given name. She'd have to keep telling people to call her Red. "Nice to meet you."

"You'll want to know no one has followed you. I circled before I picked you up," Sam said. "That's the protocol. I check the perimeter of the bus station, see who might be watching, and check if anyone is following." He watched his mirrors for a tail as he talked and drove. "There's cold water and other beverages and cheese and crackers. Make yourself comfortable and try to relax."

"Thank you."

"You're welcome. What kind of music do you like?"

"Rock."

He turned on a rock station, and she chose a bottle of chilled pineapple juice, which sounded refreshing after the heat. When was the last time she'd had pineapple juice?

"Out here, in our heat, you'll need to drink extra water. More than you think you need. Feel free to have as much as you want."

"Okay. Thanks."

The cool leather seats in the air-conditioned limo felt grand. Red leaned back, listening to the rock station, and enjoyed the taste of luxury she was getting.

Out the window, Red saw sprawling ranches and long expanses of land with mountains off in the distance.

"You can nap if you want," Sam said. "It's not a quick drive to the ranch."

"Thanks." She said the word but wasn't about to nap.

Going to sleep in a car in the middle of nowhere headed to a place I've never been, with a man I really don't know—yeah, that isn't happening. Not in this lifetime.

Instead, she watched out the window, thinking of how she'd once wanted to go out west on the back of a Harley behind her handsome new boyfriend.

She'd been a fool. Handsome as Z had been, and charming, she hadn't seen through him. Z could sell snake oil to a snake oil salesman. But beneath all that, he was as low as a snake himself. He'd slowly pulled her into his lifestyle until she'd barely recognized herself, becoming what he'd led her to believe she was. She hadn't understood the patterns she was being pulled into until it'd nearly been too late.

Out the window, she saw only road and large expanses of land on each side with clusters of tall trees here and there, beneath a blue sky. Once in a while, a ranch off in the distance.

This is wide-open country. That's good. The better to see him coming.

She'd hear his bike if he came her way, looking for her. But first, he'd have to know what direction to look. She hoped she'd done a good enough job of disappearing.

She didn't need conversation and preferred to keep to herself, so she didn't talk to Sam, just listened to the radio and watched out the windows. She'd yet to see the ranch.

Sam pulled off the road and drove the limo up beside a log guard shack with a paneled box on the outside, and then stopped. Rolling down his window, he leaned out, opened the panel door, and then took the phone receiver for a landline off the hook and dialed. "Sam, here. Am I driving all the way in?" He listened for a moment. "Okay. Will do."

She wondered who he'd been talking to, but she wasn't going to ask.

He rolled his window back up, shutting out the heat again, and then glanced over his shoulder. "Takes about fifteen to twenty minutes for Buck to get here. Buck is the ranch foreman. He's on his way. I can't take the limo all the way back there. You can get out and stretch or stay in the air conditioning—

or even take a nap. I could turn the radio down. It'll be quiet 'til he gets here."

"Don't need a nap." *What the hell is it with this nap bullshit? Does this guy really think a woman can nap out here with a stranger nearby? He's nuts.*

And he was making her nervous. She needed to walk. Her hand moved to the door handle.

CHAPTER 2

SHE COULDN'T STAY in the car. She needed to move. "I'll get out," she said. "Stretch my legs."

Sam nodded. "It's safe. If you need anything, I'm here."

"Right."

Red got out and walked a little way from the limo, and then squinted at it. She looked down the road one direction and down the road the other. She walked over to what looked like a dirt trail.

So, the ranch is at the end of this somewhere. Doesn't look like much of a road. More a dirt trail, like the ones I used to take with Charlie.

Her old high school boyfriend, who rode dirt bikes, had loved to go riding on trails, and had also had known all the places in those wooded areas to make out. She hadn't thought of him in a long time. Wondering what he'd think of the trails her life had taken since he'd moved away, another thought occurred to her.

She'd hoped Z would be a little bit like Charlie, who'd been a combination of bad boy and caring boy, as in, he would've made sure she was okay. Z was nothing but a user of women. Not even close to the kind of man her high school boyfriend had been. Red paced with her thoughts until she saw an old white truck in the midst of a dust cloud, coming toward them.

The truck came to a stop not far from the limo. Then a door opened and slammed again as a broad-shouldered man, wearing a plaid Western shirt, blue jeans, a brown leather belt with a silver buckle, and a worn pair of brown cowboy boots walked toward them. With his short dark hair, tanned skin, and salt-and-pepper mustache, he could've stepped off a movie set. He looked to be in his early sixties and carried the life he'd lived on his face and in his bearing.

Sam stepped out of the limo. "Buck, you know I don't appreciate you stirring up all this dust."

"It don't cost you much for a car wash," Buck said, one corner of his mouth kicking up. He reached his hand out to Red, not waiting for an introduction. "Buck Harris. And you must be Phoebe Adams."

"I am, but call me Red." She shook his hand with a firm grip. "Nice to meet you."

"Now, you go on and call me Buck."

"All right, Buck."

They released hands, and he reached for the suitcase Sam had removed from the trunk.

Red noted Buck's silver belt buckle with a bucking bronco on it. Likely a rodeo buckle. She hoped to learn how to ride on the ranch. If she could ride a motorcycle, she could damn sure ride a horse. But what she didn't know, he might teach her.

"Enjoy your visit here," Sam said, giving her a solemn nod.

"Thanks, I will," she said.

"Let's get a move on," Buck said, and he headed for the big old Dodge pickup truck that showed rust in places on the white paint. Clearly, a working truck.

Red followed, and Buck stopped on the passenger side and opened the truck door for her. Tall enough not to need help getting in, she climbed into his truck. "Thanks."

"You're welcome. I'll tell ya about the ranch on the way in. You ride?"

"A little."

"Good." He smiled. "That's what I like to hear. Horses, that's my life, and teaching new riders comes a close second."

Red wondered what the ranch would look like as the truck bumped along the dirt road. No pictures were allowed of the ranch to make it harder to find. No unauthorized persons were allowed entry, and it wasn't an easy ranch to find. The only people who knew the location worked here and had security clearance, or someone like a sheriff or deputy, who had reason to be there.

Z will never find me here.

The dust cloud they arrived in dissipated, and then she had a clear view of the ranch before she opened her door, not waiting for Buck to come around and get it for her. She was used to opening her own doors. Z sure as hell never would've done it for her, and he'd have given her hell for expecting it.

She stood looking at the wooden Wild West type sign with three-branded Cs across the top that announced they were here.

The house beyond it looked more like a lodge than a house. The front of the building was huge, with several gables, one big one in the front with center steps leading up to it. Made of logs, the building looked new.

"You're the second guest to arrive today," Buck said. "You'll have extra time before you're on schedule with the others, if ya want to come to the stables and ride."

"Yeah, that would be great."

"If you're a morning riser, I'm up before the sun."

She wasn't about to tell him she was a light sleeper and often woke at weird times in the early morning hours before the sun was up. This would give her something to do at those restless times, and maybe she could ride without having to do it in a group. Living in one house with so many women was really just not her thing. Communal, she was not.

She didn't like everyone knowing her business and needed time to herself. Rising early would surely accomplish that. "Thanks. And you can call me Red."

"Well, Red, after you get up tomorrow, grab you some early breakfast in the kitchen, and then come find me. I usually have a biscuit with ham on the way out the door, along with my coffee."

"Will do. Thanks, I appreciate it."

"My pleasure." He tipped his hat and took her suitcase out of the back of the truck.

At the top of the stairs in front of the house, a dark-haired, dark-skinned woman stood. "Welcome, Phoebe Adams. I'm Leah White Crane," she said. "We've been expecting you."

"I'm Red. I don't go by Phoebe."

"Well, it's nice to meet you, Red." Leah smiled. "Come on in."

She followed Leah inside and stepped into a massive great room with log walls, large wooden beams, and antler chandeliers.

"Cecelia, Phoebe is here," Leah called.

Red snorted. *Great counselor she'll be. I told her I go by Red, not Phoebe. And wouldn't that be in my file? She probably didn't even read it.*

Officer Vinson had called her by that nickname the night she'd escaped and approached him. "Come on, Red," he'd gestured to the police car. "I'll take you to the shelter. You can ride up front." But she hadn't wanted that. She'd ridden in back in case anyone who knew her saw her and reported back to Z. The officer's kindness, and the nickname, had stuck with her. It was a name Z didn't know. She hated being Phoebe. But she loved being Red. It fit her and her new life.

Irked, at being called Phoebe, Red crossed to the right side of the great room. Behind a desk, a woman with soft gray hair was sitting, typing. The woman turned toward them, smiling, and Red realized she was blind.

"Phoebe prefers to be called Red, so you'll need to update everything. Somehow, that didn't make it into her documents. Red, this is Cecelia, our secretary," Leah said.

"Pleased to meet you, Red." Cecelia reached out her hand toward Red.

Red shook her hand. "Nice to meet ya."

"Now, you just ignore the things that have your name wrong until I get them fixed," Cecelia said. "I'll be right on that."

"She's a fast typist," Leah said. "It won't take long."

"If you need anything," Cecelia said, "either stop by my desk or call the private line." Cecelia placed her hand on a card on her desk. "There's a phone in your room if you need to call out, and please memorize this number, so you'll have an emergency number to call if you leave the property."

"Thank you." Red took the card, amazed at how self-sufficient Cecelia was. She didn't have to look at anything to know where it was.

"I like to know when you leave the property, so

please check in with me if you go out. I worry if I don't know where my people are."

Great. Are they going to keep tabs on everything we do?

Red rolled her eyes.

"She can't see your response, Red," Leah said softly.

"Oh," Red said, blushing. "Sure."

"Very good. Now, here's your key." Cecelia reached into a drawer and pulled out a key. Smiling, she held out the key. "You have your pick of the guest rooms, except for two, which already have names on the doors."

"Okay," Red said. "Thanks."

"You're welcome." Cecelia's phone rang. "We'll chat later. I'm looking forward to it." She picked up the phone. "Hello, Three Cs. This is Cecelia."

"I'll show you the rooms," Leah said. "Then you can settle in. Later, I'll take you on a tour of the grounds."

"Okay." Red followed Leah through the great room to a hallway that went back a long way. Rooms were on each side, just like hotel rooms, and the unclaimed rooms had their doors open so she could see inside as they walked past.

"Which room would you like?" Leah asked. "They

all have the same amenities; the only difference will be in the view."

"Is the center going to be full?" What she really wanted was a quiet room away from anyone else.

"Yes, by the end of this week," Leah said.

So, none of the rooms were going to be more private than any of the others. Red picked one and walked inside. "This will do."

"Good. I'll tell Cecelia which room you're in and have your bag brought in," Leah said. "Find me when you're ready for me to show you around."

"Okay," Red said.

Leah closed the door, giving her the room all to herself. *Privacy. Finally. Better enjoy that now. Before all those other women get here.*

The room had an outer wall made of logs and three dry-walls decorated with framed quilt pieces all done in yellow, gold, red, and green. A matching quilt covered the big queen-sized bed that had a large wooden headboard and footboard made of logs. A large window looked out over a great view of the ranch and the mountains beyond. She walked over to it to see if it opened. It did not.

Won't be going out that way. But then, no one will be coming in that way, either. She walked back to the door and checked it. Just a normal lock, like any house would have. *Z could bust right through that.* But he'd have to come all the way through the lobby and the hall to reach her door. She locked the door, and then looked back at the window, only now fully taking in the impressive view. *But he'll have one hell of a time finding me here. Inside the room, knowing she was safe, and where no one could see her, she finally let down her guard and relaxed. She couldn't remember that last time she'd done that.*

After a shower and a twenty-minute nap, Red found Leah in the great room.

"You look more rested," Leah said with a smile.

"Yeah, I am."

"Are you hungry or thirsty?"

"Yeah." She shrugged. "A little."

"Then we'll go see our cook, Emma Ives, first. George Ives is our maintenance man. They used to be at one of the big ski lodges, but he had heart surgery and retired from the lodge. They wanted a quiet, less hectic lifestyle."

A large stone fireplace stood on one kitchen wall, and a restaurant-sized stove stood on the other, with a matching double-sided refrigerator on the third. The room also had a kitchen island and a bar with stools combo. A humming, brown-haired women turned and saw them. "Hello," the older woman said. "Now, who's hungry?"

Leah laughed. "Emma is always trying to feed us. Emma, I'd like you to meet Phoebe who prefers to be called Red."

"Hello, Red." Emma stuck out her hand, and Red shook it. "Pleased to meet you."

"Nice to meet you, too," Red said.

"When was your last meal?"

Red paused, thinking. "At the second bus stop."

"What did you have?"

"A hot dog and fries."

"Been a while since you had a real meal then." Emma moved to the oven.

"What's our snack tonight?" Leah asked.

"Chocolate chip cookies," Emma said. The aroma now filled the room, making Red's mouth water.

"Buck ate the last ones pretty fast," Leah said.

"He does that, and then says there's no food in this house." Emma shook her head. "That man. It's not like he ever goes hungry."

"What's for dinner tonight, Emma?"

"Well now, that depends." She looked at Red. "Do you have any food allergies?"

Red shook her head. "No."

"Good, then tonight it's pork chops and fried

potatoes. Just wanted to make sure you weren't allergic to pork. I had chicken for Plan B. We'll have it, tomorrow night."

"Sounds good," Leah said.

Emma poured glasses of milk for Red and Leah and set them on the bar. Looking at Red, she said, "Now, tell me your favorite pie."

"Cherry."

"I believe I can work a cherry pie in one night while you're here. Just need to get some cherries." She smiled at Red.

"Uh that would be great, thanks." *Everyone here is so nice.* Red wasn't used to all this niceness. She picked a cookie off the plate Emma set in front of them and took a bite.

Holy mother of sweetness! This is the best damn chocolate chip cookie I've ever had. No wonder everyone here is so sweet with Emma kept feeding them like this. A few more of these and I'll be in a sugar coma.

They ate two more cookies, and then Leah said, "We're off on the tour now. See you at dinner, Emma. These cookies were great."

"Yeah, great," Red mumbled, finishing the last of her third and final cookie.

"Next, I'll show you the pool," Leah said.

A set of French doors to the fanciest pool Red

had ever seen. A tall, outdoor, free-standing fireplace wall made of oval gray stones stood on one side, and the other sides were bordered by tall stone planters with leafy green plants.

"Damn, skippy," she said. "This is one nice set up."

"The same man who built the fireplaces inside the house designed these. The pool is heated, so we can swim in winter and then warm up by the fireplace when we get out," Leah said. "I'm looking forward to that."

"Yeah, I would be too, if I was here in winter."

"The pool is always open for you to use during any free time in the day or in the evening. Next, I'll we'll head to the stables."

Passing the pool, they walked to the stables, leaving the main house behind.

"We get good exercise here," Leah said, "just walking."

"Yeah, why are the buildings so far apart?" Red asked.

"Why not?" Leah spread her arms. "Look around you. Everything you can see from here is ranch land."

"I'm used to buildings being closer together."

"In the cities, they are. But out here, they don't have to be. Out here, there's room to breathe."

"Yeah, there sure is." Red took in the views all around her. "It's nice."

"There you are," Buck said, riding up to where the fence stood just outside the barn. "I was wonderin' when you two would be by to see me this afternoon."

Buck sat atop a large red horse. Red looked up at the man and horse, thinking a big horse like that suited him.

"And here we are." Leah's cell phone rang. She looked at it and frowned. Saying, "Excuse me," she put the phone to her ear and walked away from them.

Buck stepped down off his horse. "Come on," he said. "I'll introduce you to the other horses."

"I'd like that." Pleased to be meeting the horses, she smiled, ducking her head, her pleasure a private thing.

He gave her a kind look and said, "You can help me feed 'em if you want."

"Oh yeah, I want to feed them."

"I'll be teaching the others how to care for our horses, along with the riding lessons, but there's no reason you can't start now. Be a few days before they're all here."

"I'd like that." She wrinkled her nose. "I'm not

really much of a group person."

He gave her a keen look, a quiet pause, and then said, "I'm here early every morning. Help me get 'em ready in the morning, and I'll let you ride. You're welcome any time."

Yeah, that's a much better plan than lessons with a bunch of other women. She kept that thought to herself. "I'll be here every morning." She nodded. "Thanks."

They went into the barn, and Red began to meet the horses. By the time Leah had rejoined them, Red had already picked out which horse she wanted to ride. She couldn't wait until tomorrow morning.

The women headed to the gun range next. The range was outdoors, well away from other buildings, and right out in the open. The open-sided building, which looked like a long rectangular shaded picnic shelter, was equipped with tables to place guns and ammo on, lined up in a row. Targets were set a distance away.

"The range is used by appointment only, and only with a trained instructor accompanying you," Leah said. "We'll be starting with gun safety and intro to handguns classes. Every woman who leaves here will know how a gun works and how to operate one."

"I already know about guns."

"Do you carry?"

"No." She shook her head hard, thinking of what Z could do to her if she had a gun he could take away.

Leah, noting her expression, said, "All guns on Three Cs Ranch are accounted for at all times. Your instructor will bring handguns and take them with him when he goes. Buck has rifles. There are no guns in the main house. They're all at Buck's place. When borrowing a gun from one of the men, they know the responsibility for that gun lies with them, even if it's in your hands. They keep tight rein on those guns. For your safety."

"That's a damn good thing."

"Have you ever heard a gun go off?"

"Uh, yeah." Her tone held that "Do you think I'm stupid?" tone that had gotten her smacked in the ear once by Z.

"Range times are scheduled and posted on the chalkboard beside the door leading out to the pool. Everyone will know when those guns are going off. Is gunfire a trigger for you?"

"Naw."

"That's good. If you hear a shot at night, that's Buck with one of the long guns, likely is shooting at a coyote. Buck was a sheriff's deputy and is a Marine veteran. He assists in our gun classes."

"Cool." Red liked the fact that Buck had worked as a deputy and knew how to shoot. Unlike Z, Red did not hate cops. But then, she'd never been out to break the law.

∽

THE NEXT MORNING, Red went to meet Buck in the kitchen as he was grabbing coffee and a biscuit with ham that Emma had made for him. They both looked at her, surprise showing in Emma's raised eyebrows.

"Mornin', Red," Buck said jovially.

"Morning." Not the morning person Buck was, Red's response was a mumble.

"Oh hun, you want some coffee and a biscuit?" Emma reached for a coffee cup.

"Make hers to go, Emma. She's comin' out to the barn with me."

"Oh, you are?" Emma smiled. "That's nice. I'll fix you right up in a jiffy."

Soon, Red and Buck were on their way to the barn, carrying their "first" breakfast. It was still dark outside, making her feel like she should still be in bed sleeping. Thankfully, Buck didn't try to talk to her before she'd had her first morning coffee.

Once inside the barn, they finished their biscuits, and Buck showed her his morning routine for taking care of the horses. Then it was time for her first lesson, and she watched as he saddled a horse with a gold coat and white mane and tail.

"This mare's name is Sunshine. She's a palomino. She's gentle and easy to ride. Now, put your left hand on the saddle and your left foot in the stirrup and then—"

She stepped up and threw her right leg over the horse as if she'd been riding all her life.

Ah hell this is easy, she thought. *Like mounting a Harley.*

"Well, you know how." He stood holding the reins and handed them to her. "Just walk around the corral for a minute, and I'll tell you what you're doing wrong."

She stared silently, without not willing to tell him she didn't know what to do next.

"What are you waiting for, Red? Put your heels in her side and tell her to giddy up."

Gently, Red nudged the horse's sides with her bootheels. Sunshine started slowly walking around the paddock.

Red kept her nervousness to herself, along with

her fear. She knew better than to ever let anyone see that.

The minute you let someone see your weaknesses was the minute you handed them a way to control you and hurt you.

"Make her go a little faster," came Buck's gruff voice. "Give her another jab in the ribs."

Red gave the jab with her heels, and Sunshine picked up her pace, which made Red a little more nervous. This was a big horse she sat on, a lot higher up than a Harley.

"That's fast enough. You don't want to run her just yet."

They moved around the corral for a few more minutes, and then Buck said, "I got to mend some fence line. You ready to take a short ride? That path right there?" he said, pointing. "It's an easy path to Whisper Creek. It's nice and quiet there."

Feeling more confident now that she'd managed not to fall off the horse, she nodded. "Yes, sir." She had respect for Buck and wanted to show it. "I'd like that."

He nodded. "I'll let you out." Then he headed for the gate and opened it for her.

She rode Sunshine through the gate and down the path toward the creek. The morning sun was up, and birds chirped. Into the trees and further down the path, it got quieter. They followed the trail until they reached the creek.

At the creek, the horse stopped. Red dismounted and, still holding the reins, waited while Sunshine drank from the creek.

She stood taking in the sights and sounds. Even closed her eyes to listen.

This was nice, right here. Real nice.

After a while, her stomach growled. It was time to head back. She needed that second breakfast.

Mounting Sunshine again, she turned the horse back to the trail, which lead home to the barn. Halfway there, Red started to get more impatient.

She's a nice horse but this is too damn slow.

Her stomach growled again. Red dug her heels in hard.

Sunshine moved into a fast trot, and Red bounced up and down in the saddle, smacking the saddle hard.

"Damn, girl, slow down!" she yelled. Her butt bounced up and down in the saddle, her boots fell out of the stirrups, and then she bounced off the saddle, falling hard onto the ground.

Sunshine trotted on down the trail.

CHAPTER 3

RED CAME to as Buck knelt over her.

"What happened, Red?" Concern filled his eyes as he checked her over. "Sunshine came back to the barn without ya, so I came looking."

Her head and her ankle hurt, along with her pride. "I, she, no, it must've been bees. Damn bees." She frowned.

He raised an eyebrow, clearly skeptical, but didn't say anything. Then he helped her sit up and checked her head for lumps. "Must've hit your head here," he said.

She reached for her head where the lump was and felt the raised place. *Damn. That hurts.*

"Come on, let's get you back to the lodge," Buck said. "I got my Jeep."

"Okay." She let him help her up and into the Jeep, as she was still feeling light-headed.

"Emma will have breakfast ready and waiting. If you're feeling hungry…"

"I'm very hungry."

"That's a good sign," he said.

Once in the Jeep, Red said, "That trail ride was nice…before the bees. Quiet. I needed that."

"Glad you enjoyed it. Hang on, and I'll try not to bounce you around too much with this Jeep."

"Thank you," she said, relieved.

Back at the lodge, breakfast was on the table, and Emma was waiting for them, worried frown on her face. "What happened?" she asked Buck the minute they entered.

How does she know something happened? Nobody knew but Buck and me. He didn't call anyone since he found me. Is she gonna be in everybody's business? Good thing I made Buck promise not to tell anyone about my private morning riding lessons.

"It's not like you to be this late for breakfast," Emma said. "Have a seat. Eggs are gonna get cold."

Red let go a relieved breath. So, her concern hadn't been because anyone had seen her fall.

Scrambled eggs, biscuits and gravy, and ham were

set on the table, along with a pitcher of orange juice. It all looked delicious. Red took a seat, hoping they could all just eat and forget about what happened. She had a lump on the head, but it wasn't the end of the world.

"I will as soon as I have a word with Leah," Buck said.

Leah looked up from the table and stood.

Red reached for the eggs and tried to look nonchalant while keeping her thoughts to herself. *Damn. Buck is gonna tell Leah.*

After they spoke, Leah came back in and said, "Red, step outside with me for a minute."

Red rolled her eyes. "Fine." She stood and followed Leah out of the room.

The other woman's gaze locked Red's expression. "Tell me what happened."

"I was riding to the creek, and horse must've ridden into a bunch of bees 'cause the next thing I knew, I was on the ground."

"Bees," she repeated, her dark gaze narrowing.

Red felt a blush heat her cheeks. "Yeah, bees."

"When Buck found you, you were out, probably because you'd hit your head. He doesn't know how long you were out."

"Yeah, I don't know either, but I'm fine."

"We're still going to have to take you in to town to the emergency room to have you checked out."

Red stiffened. "No, I don't need to go."

Leah's expression hardened. "It's the policy for head injuries. You need to be checked for a possible concussion. We're not taking any chances."

Red's shoulders slumped. "Well, damn, let a girl eat first at least."

"You're feeling okay? And you're hungry?"

"Yes and yes. Damn. Now, can I just eat?"

"Yes, but soon as breakfast is over, be ready to go."

Red's gaze fell away. "I can't go to the hospital. I don't have insurance."

Leah sighed. "Most of the women who come here won't have insurance. A few of the local doctors donate services, if needed."

"Wow. That's generous."

"Yes, it is. Now let's go back in and eat so we can get you on the road to the hospital."

Back at the table, Leah reached for the gravy, and said, "Now, that we're all here." She looked at Buck and smiled. "Every morning, we'll have breakfast together, family style." She turned to Red. "There will be eight of you."

Red noticed two women at the table whom she hadn't met.

"Red, I'd like you to meet Karla and Neecy."

"Nice to meet you," Karla and Neecy both said.

Red nodded at them as she took another biscuit. "You, too."

"Janelle gets in tonight, and Karla, Tamara, Ellen and Chyna will be here in the next few days. Then we'll start having group sessions."

Oh joy, Red thought. *Where we get to share all our back closet stuff that we really don't want to talk about.*

"Dinner will be served in the main dining room, but all other meals and snacks will be here."

"Wait 'til you see the custom dining room furniture," Karla said, smiling. "It's hand-carved. Tell her the story, Leah."

"Our table was donated by a custom furniture maker and cabinet designer," Leah said. "Each chair has the Three Cs' brand on the back. And if you were to turn the chairs over, you'd see the furniture maker's mark as well. He said he'd never make another set exactly like this one. So, it's unique in the world. He asked us to remind every woman who comes here that they, too, are unique in the world."

"Isn't that cool?" Karla said.

"Yeah." Red took another bite of ham. "Real cool."

She'd been in the dining area situated on the left side of the large great room and had seen it's log walls and heavy wooden beams from which hung antler candelabras. The long, rectangular, dining room table, with its many tall chairs, seated fourteen and had to be the furniture Karla was talking about.

The great room was pretty awesome, too, with a leather couch and two leather love seats. Everything in the oversized, open room was a shade of brown or cream, and appeared soft, warm, and inviting. A large stone fireplace, which reached all the way to the tall ceiling, was on one wall. There was also a library and computer. Anything she needed to do online would have to be accomplished within the rules of the center. Anything other than looking up topics online, she'd have to run past Cecelia, who would make sure she wasn't traceable on the other end through any communications sent. Emails went out over an encrypted system. All social media sites were blocked.

Leah turned to Red. "I need to do your intake interview tomorrow, for our records. And in the event they replace me, so the next therapist can step right in without you having to go over everything again. We can talk, tomorrow."

Red nodded. She'd known she'd have to start all

over with counseling after she arrived here and was surprised the subject had waited until now.

After breakfast, George Ives, the maintenance man and Emma's husband, drove Red to the hospital. Karla and Neecy rode along.

At the ER, they waited for what seemed like forever. The doctor ran a bunch of tests on her, and then proclaimed her concussion free, so they headed back to the ranch.

∼

THE NEXT MORNING, after her private riding lesson with Buck and second breakfast, Leah came up to Red.

"Come to my office, and we'll do your intake."

Red suppressed a groan. Barely. "Okay."

"If I'm in private session, the sign saying so will be on the door. When you see that, go and tell Cecelia you want to see me when I'm out, and she'll get any messages to me."

Inside the private session room was a leather couch, two leather chairs, and stained-glass lamps near each. The effect was warm and inviting.

"Have a seat," Leah said as she sat behind her big desk. "You know, Cecelia wasn't always blind."

"Oh. What happened to her?"

"She was savagely attacked outside a mall in Detroit. She came to us from the Rosewood Center in North Carolina." Leah dropped her voice to a whisper. "You don't want to whisper near her, because she'll hear you anyway."

"Okay," Red said.

Leah leaned back and steepled her fingers. "Okay, tell me what happened to make you run to the center. Start at the beginning and don't leave anything out."

Red took a breath and launched into the story of her and Z. By the time she was done, she was tired and wanted nothing more than to go take a nap. And Red never napped.

~

Once all the women had arrived at the ranch, their classes started.

Every morning, their schedule stated that they'd begin with physical training, and then halfway through the class they'd switch to self-defense. They'd practice on each other.

Barrett, their new defensive instructor pulled a

piece of paper out of his pocket and unfolded it. "Let's start with roll call, so I know your names."

He called out the names, and each woman identified herself.

"Very good," Barrett said, putting the paper away. "You're going to work with each other, woman on woman, the first few days. Later, I'll bring in my guys from the team."

"Oh." Chyna's eyes widened. Then she frowned. "I don't know about that. I'm not very strong. To go up against a larger man…" She shook her head.

Chyna was like a little mouse. The helpless kind of woman who got on Red's nerves. She'd already noticed the way Chyna seemed star struck by their self-defense instructor. And she'd had enough of the woman's "poor little me" routine.

"Don't be stupid," Red said. "You've got to. How are we gonna learn to fight off a man if we only practice on women?" She gestured to the group. "None of these girls looks like they could kick my ass or like they'd even want to."

"*Women*," Barrett said. "And you'd be surprised the damage even a small female fighter can do, especially if she's trained. Even boxers don't usually box outside their weight class. There's no shame in being afraid of someone bigger or stronger than you. But you're going to learn the moves, and learn them well, before we have anyone my size coming at you. We'll lay the groundwork, and we'll build on what you know."

Well, he just has all the answers, doesn't he? But he hasn't been clear on what we'll be learning. She raised a hand, and then scowled because she wasn't a school kid and dropped her hand. "Are we gonna learn kickboxing? Karate? What exactly are you going to teach us?" Red asked. "And what are your credentials? You got a black belt or something beyond those big muscles?"

She didn't like men who strode into the room and then took over. Like Z. Like this guy. He'd better give her a reason she should listen to him.

Unfazed, he answered, "I'm trained in karate, judo, taekwondo, aikido, jujitsu, boxing and kickboxing. And yes, I'm a 4th degree black belt, as well as a former Green Beret."

Damn. A Green Beret. That's intense. Her respect for Barrett rose a bit higher.

"Ladies, this training isn't going to be from one focused discipline. I'm going to teach you elements from each, appropriate to your skill and fitness level, which can help you in a fight, but we're not going to worry about what we call it, other than self-defense."

Now we're talking. That's what I need, good training.

"All right," she said. "Long as I can kick the guy's ass, I don't care what you call it. I'm in."

"Good." Barrett faced the class. "Listen up. We're going to start every morning with conditioning. A jog to warm up followed by jumping jacks. Then push-ups, sit ups, squats, planks, a few yoga stretches, and tai chi. That's the first half-hour, and then the second half-hour, we'll work on self-defense."

He's got to be kidding.

"Just thirty minutes for self-defense?" Red said. "Not a full hour? I don't need all that PT. I can jog on my own, without some class."

"How far do you run every day?" Barrett asked.

Red shook her head and crinkled her nose. She wasn't about to admit she didn't exercise. She'd never needed to. Working on her feet at the bar or restaurant she worked off whatever weight she might've added. Being on your feet all day instead of sitting on your ass tended to do that.

He arched an eyebrow. "We're working out together as a unit. Some of you may be at difference fitness levels, and that's fine. You'll all get faster at PT the more we do, and I'll add on and change things as necessary." He paused and looked around the room. "Now, I want to make it clear that it's not my job as your instructor, nor my mission, to make you stronger. That job is up to you. How much you get out of these classes is up to you. I'll take you from where you are now; using strengths you already have, to where you can use those strengths to defend yourself. Your endurance may improve, and your strength may improve, and that's a plus. The goal here is for you to be able to defend yourself today and any day you walk out that door." He pointed to the door. "I guarantee that when you walk out that door, you'll know more about self-defense than when you walked in. Beyond that, how far you take it is up to you."

Leah White Crane had perched on a chair behind them and was watching him and nodding. She'd told them she'd come and go and would stay handy in case anything triggered one of them.

"All right," Barrett said, "line up, and we'll start our jog. I'll be working out with you. This isn't a race or a marathon. This is just to get your heart rate going and warm you up."

"I'm already warm," Judy said in a low voice.

Brown-haired, freckle-faced Judy fanned herself, and Tamara, beside her, giggled. Chyna, looking at Barrett with star in her eyes, giggled and blushed.

Red rolled her eyes.

That one is so gone, if he tells her to stand on her head and howl like dog, she'll do it. She's making a fool of herself. I'm never gonna be that gone on a guy.

Barrett ran with them, and then had them do jumping jacks and sit-ups. In-between sit-ups and planks, he asked, "How many of you have an exercise routine?"

No one raised a hand.

Neecy-Lynn said, "I had a gym membership, but I only went the first two weeks, and then I got busy at the salon." She waved a hand, which had deep purple nail polish on her long fingernails. "I ended up canceling it."

"By the end of the month when you leave, you'll have this routine, and it's one you can do anywhere," he said. "No equipment or gym membership needed. Repeat a pattern for thirty days, and it easily becomes a habit. Now, I want you to think about habits and routines. Habits can be healthy, such as exercise," he said.

Habits made her think of Z.

"I had a habit who tried to break me, but I showed him," Red said. "Ain't any habit I can't break."

Ignoring her comment, Barrett showed them how to do a plank, then had them lower to the ground and support their weight on their arms while they held their bodies as stiff as "planks", and then he set the timer. They had to hold the plank until the timer went off. Everyone got into position.

Red watched Chyna line up in front of Barrett and how he turned his attention back to the group, looking at each of them. *That girl is gonna make a fool out of herself if she falls for him but looks like it's too late.*

"Let's think about the difference between habits and routines," he said. "A routine can be something a stalker, or anyone watching you, can pick up on quickly. We need to vary our routines while maintaining our habits. So, let's say you did go to a gym and got in the routine of going Monday, Wednesday and Friday at five-thirty on those days. You could change that time and go early in the morning instead. Change things around. Vary the days and times you go. Park in a different spot, go through a different door. Think of ways you can vary your routines, so they don't become such set patterns that someone watching you can predict your behavior."

Red had to admit the man was fit. And hard to keep up with.

The timer he set rang. "Push-ups are next," he said.

Chyna groaned.

"All right," he said. "You've all done well for your first day. It'll get easier, and I'll add to it. Now, everyone, get some water, and then we're going to talk about situational awareness."

They got water bottles and sat down. Red sat in the back in her own row, giving herself some space from the other women.

"Situational awareness, also known as situation awareness, or SA, is a military term, the concept of which goes back to Sun Tzu's *The Art of War* before the concept had a modern name. These terms were first used during the First World War. Simply put, it's observing your environment and the people within it and anticipating what they might do." Barrett looked around at each of the women as he spoke.

Red was too busy drinking water to make any comments. She had a dry tickle in her throat and didn't want to cough. The sooner they moved through all this talking, and started fighting, the better.

"How many of you have heard of an OODA Loop?" he asked and glanced around. "None of you? Okay. The OODA loop is the decision cycle of observe, orient, decide, and act, developed by U.S.

Air Force Colonel John Boyd." He wrote OODA on the chalkboard and above it wrote situational awareness. Then he turned back to them. "Situational awareness is the first tool in your self-defense tool kit, and you're going to learn how to practice it every day."

So, he's gonna give us all this classwork instead of teaching us hands on?

"I just want to learn to kick ass," Red said. "I don't need a history lesson."

Barrett ignored her and pressed on. "In combat, the winning strategy is to 'get inside' your opponent's OODA loop by making your decisions faster, but also by having a better situational awareness than your opponent, and even changing the situation in ways your opponent can't monitor or comprehend. Losing your situational awareness is being 'out of the loop'. So, you want to be aware at all times and not be out of that loop and taken by surprise."

"Yeah, you got to stay aware, 'cause if you don't," Red smacked her hands together, making a loud noise, "bam, upside of the head." She made a face at Barrett. "So, tell me something new. Hell, I learned that when I was five."

"We're laying a foundation here," he said. "Foundation first, and then brick by brick, so no bricks are missing."

Red folded her arms and leaned back. "Wake me when there's something new."

Addressing Red, he said, "Tell me the number on your house."

I need a number. I'll use my old apartment.

"Five three one one, why?"

"Now tell me the number on the center here."

"Ain't one."

"And the number on the bus terminal?"

She shrugged, not knowing it.

"Here's a homework assignment for you all this week. When you go out, in to town or just out anywhere, observe the number of the building every time you go inside. This will provide you with an address in case you need to call law enforcement or an ambulance or fire truck. This is a practice for you to get into. Any questions?"

"Yeah," Red said. "I've got one. A big one. We're here at this center, where there aren't any numbers, and there aren't any other buildings around here that have numbers. Not for miles. So where are we gonna practice this homework, when we aren't allowed to leave?"

CHAPTER 4

"That's a good question," Barrett said.

Leah, who'd stepped in to observe, said, "I have the answer to that one. We've planned an outing to town on Saturday to shop for anything you might've forgotten to bring, or if you don't need anything, to show you the area in case you ever want to drive to town. I don't know where you got the idea that you can't leave. Of course, you can, any time you want."

"Good." Red perked up.

"What you can't do is leave the program, and then come back," Leah said. "If you walk away from the program, another woman will take your place, and as you know, there's a waiting list. We can't hold your spot for you. So, you have to commit to the program. Nowhere have we said you can't leave the property. Going to town is no problem. You can even go by yourself, later, if you want. Buck will let you borrow a car if he's not using it. We just want to keep you safe when you do go out. Part of what you'll learn in this class is how to be safe when you leave here, and we're starting this week."

"Thank you, Leah," Barrett said. "We'll talk more about situational awareness tomorrow and start some drills for that. I'm bringing my guys in tomorrow to help with the drills."

"You're bringing in other guys already?" Tamara said, her expression fearful.

"We only have three days to get you ready for Saturday, counting today, so we'll start right in. You'll be learning fast, but nothing really physical. I need them to help me watch what you're doing and make corrections, and we'll demonstrate what we want you to do."

"I don't mind a little full contact," Red said.

"It'll be weeks before anyone goes full contact. We're laying that foundation with bricks, remember?"

"Yeah, yeah." She shrugged.

"Tomorrow will be more intention drills, and I'll add on."

They'd picked names out of a hat for their

workout partners, and Red had drawn Chyna's name. Just her luck to get the mouse with the crush on their instructor.

"Back to situational awareness," Barrett said. "This is the foundation. I want you to carry it everywhere and be aware of your surroundings at all times."

Red nodded and began making notes in her notebook.

"When you're aware of your surroundings, there's less chance of surprise. If there's surprise, there may be more distance, and distance can be to your advantage. Now, here's one more thing to add to that assignment," he said.

Red looked up at him, pen poised, but he looked at another woman. Emma had come to the door and waved at him. He didn't wave back but continued. "Every time you enter a building, note the exits, just like you'd look for the fire exits in a theater or the exits in an airplane. Get into the habit of finding them when you walk in, so you can find them easily and quickly. You can start practicing here on the ranch before you go into town on Saturday." He nodded. "That's enough for today. I believe Emma has breakfast waiting."

"You joining us?" Red asked.

"You're welcome to join us for breakfast," Leah said.

"Thank you, but not today," Barrett said.

"Well, you're welcome any time," Leah said. "Open invitation for you and your team."

"We appreciate that." He smiled. "I have to get on back to the main office for a meeting," he said, "but I'll see you all tomorrow, bright and early."

Everyone filed out and headed for breakfast. Today's menu was French toast with warm maple syrup, sausage links, and sliced apples in cinnamon. More sugar than Red ate in a week by the time she added orange juice.

CHAPTER 5

TODAY WAS the second day of self-defense training. Red watched a handsome man walk into the room, following Barrett. With his short dark hair and freshly shaved chin, he had a clean-cut military look that could've been straight out of a magazine or TV ad for recruiting. The complete opposite of the type of men Red had been hanging around with recently.

He had a tan, muscular toned body that moved in a powerful way and his dark brown eyes glanced at her briefly.

He's quiet, Red thought. *And damn hot.*

Barrett introduced him as one of the Brotherhood Protectors. Tim "Timbers" Watson, former USMC Staff sergeant.

What the hell kind of name is 'Timbers'?

Barrett said, "Today, we're going to do intention drills." He held up a soft thick black knife. "This is a Nok knife, used for training." He handed it to Red. "Pass it around. I want each of you to hold it before we begin, so you can see it's harmless."

The women passed the knife around.

"We're going to take turns with this drill. One of you comes into the center."

Barrett gestured to Red.

She joined him, and he handed her the knife.

"Put it in your waistband."

She followed his orders.

He continued. "The rest of you are going to join us here in the center. I want you to walk around as if you were in a crowd, moving through a mall or another populated area. Those without the knife will try to grab the knife and run. Red, your job is to try to notice them before they get the knife."

"Got it," Red said.

"The rest of you, one at a time, try to get the knife without being detected. Some of you will bluff, and some of you will be after the knife. Got it?"

The others nodded yes.

Red said, "What do you want me to do when I catch them?"

"We're not getting into fight scenarios today. We're focusing only on awareness."

Red frowned. *Too much talking and too little fighting.*

She glanced at Timbers, wondering what he thought of this training. He'd been watching her but turned his attention back to Barrett who was still speaking. Distracted by his profile she forced herself to listen and focus on the training.

Barrett said, "Now, we're going to do a drill, which is about reading the intentions of the person approaching you. You'll stand here, and each person will approach you in turn. One may be friendly and reach out to shake your hand, the next may be faking it and reach out to grab you. Red, your job is to watch for signs and listen to your intuition. When you think the person has bad intentions, hold up your hand and say, 'Stop'. When you think the person has good intentions, you'll shake their hand. Got it?"

"Yep," she said.

"Any questions?"

"Nope."

No one had any questions. They started the exercise.

Timbers came toward her. Would he reach for the knife or shake her hand and be harmless? She couldn't read him at all. The minute he got close enough to hurt her she said, "Stop."

His hand came toward her. "Nice to meet you," he said, and winked.

Damn. Her face colored. "Nice to meet you," she mumbled.

They drilled this exercise again and again.

Every time someone came toward her, she assigned a bad intention. *There it was, that hyper alert shit, Leah talked about.* Where the others couldn't pick out the bad guys, Red couldn't pick out the good ones.

Timbers would be a good poker player. Everything about him was quiet, from the way he moved, to the way he watched to the way he spoke. Few of the women read him right more than once. *I always thought marines were louder. Maybe that's when they aren't in attack or watch mode.*

Finally they were done and Barrett said, "You did well today, for a first attempt. The more you practice, the better you'll get."

"I hope so," Red said with frustration. Far from naïve like Chyna and a few of the other women, who couldn't read bad intentions, she was the complete opposite. What the hell had Z done to her head? She hardly recognized herself. And it made her want to hit something. Hard.

"You will," he said. "We'll be working today's exercises into next week. Then on Monday, I'll add a new topic."

"When do I get to punch somebody?" Red asked. "You know, real world stuff."

His face grew stern. "Situational awareness *is* real world stuff. SA has saved my life and my men's lives."

Timbers quiet unreadable gaze was on her.

"Who are you mad at, Red? Is there someone you want to hit?" Tamara asked.

That is none of her damn business.

"He ain't here, and I want to do more than hit him," Red said. "What about the gun range? When do we get to shoot?"

"Beginning shooter lessons will be in the third week. First, you'll need to learn how to keep someone from taking your gun. Too often, handguns are used against their owners, and that's the last thing you'd want to have happen. Just think, if someone can get this knife away from you," Barrett said, "what will they do if it's a gun? A weapon is no good to you if he takes it away. We won't add guns until week three."

Chyna winced. "I don't know about shooting a gun. I don't think I'm up for that."

Red rolled her eyes. She started gathering her stuff, exasperated with mouse girl.

Not up for that. What did she come here for? We all knew what the program involved when we signed up. She has to learn to shoot guns and I have to take classes with these women. She needs to suck it up like I have to.

"Have you ever been around guns or anyone who knew how to shoot?" Barrett asked.

Chyna said, "My ex and his cousins. They all hunt. But at the cabin, they drink and shoot guns. They're so loud. I always go into the cabin when they do that because it's scary. I'm kind of afraid of guns."

Red turned her head, tired of watching them. *Z and his men carried guns. Hell, their women sometimes carried. But even if they didn't, they knew how to shoot. With men like that in the world, you'd better learn how to shoot back. Chyna wouldn't last a day in that world.*

"I can get you over that fear. By the end of week three, you'll be shooting as well as any other beginner."

"I just don't know about that. I'm not ready."

Leah had come to watch the last exercise and had been sitting quietly as she watched. She cleared her throat. "We can talk about that in session. Ladies, when we have late morning group sessions, we can discuss any issues relating to anything that arises in the class. I'll always come in for the last ten minutes of class for anyone who might need me."

"Thank you," Chyna said.

"Afraid we'll lose our shit?" Red put her hands on her hips. "We're not the crazy ones. Most of us didn't start a thing. Why don't our exes have to go through therapy? The judge could make them."

"Enforced therapy is often ineffective because the patient doesn't want to change," Leah said. "There's little anyone can do to make an adult change if they don't want to."

"My ex could make any woman change," Red said. "If she doesn't, she's likely to wind up dead."

Timbers gaze was still on her. She turned her head not wanting anyone's attention right now, even his.

"Ladies, our time is up," Barrett said, drawing their attention again. "Your new assignment is to find where the exits are and mark in your minds where the doors are as soon as you walk into a building. Again, this would be helpful in case of a fire, as well as escaping a predator. That exercise, and remembering the numbers on a building, are your homework assignments for this week."

"Is everyone ready for Saturday?" Leah asked. "You'll have one more day to train and learn, so if you have any questions about what you've learned so far or thoughts about Saturday, bring them tomorrow."

⁓

SATURDAY ARRIVED, and the women all went into town. Leah and Barrett accompanied the group as the women got to shop and practice the homework. Red wondered where Timbers was, but then heard Barrett tell one of the others that he was out of town on another assignment.

Now, they'd be allowed to leave the property and run errands or explore on their own. Each had to memorize the number of the shelter, and they were quizzed to make sure they knew it.

⁓

BARRETT AND TIMBERS carried in training bags and

set eight of them up in a row along with sets of boxing gloves.

"Today, you're going to learn kickboxing moves, for conditioning and to add another skill set to your self-defense kit," Timbers said.

Barrett said, "Questions?" His gaze swung to Chyna and narrowed. "Chyna, what do you think?"

Red rolled her eyes at "mouse girl", knowing she'd complain.

Her mouth pursed. "I think I'm not strong enough to box," she said. "That's for strong men or women who have muscles. I'm not strong like that. I'm small-boned."

Oh, give me a break, Red thought as she listened to Chyna. *Doing the poor little save-me routine "sugar", or are you really that helpless?*

"You're stronger than you think," Barrett said. "Don't give up on it. Give it a try, and let's see how you do."

"I can't give up." Chyna shook her head. "When I leave here, I have to be ready to defend myself when Phineas or his cousins, or anyone else from his family, comes looking for me."

"Phineas is your ex?" Barrett asked.

She nodded. "Yes, but he usually goes by the name of Finn."

"You said when, not if," Barrett said. "What makes you so sure they'll come looking?"

"It's not something I can explain. I just know him, and I know his family. None of them is happy about me walking around, able to share family secrets. They're real big on keeping those family secrets locked up."

His eyes softened. "I'll prepare you the best I can for any kind of attacker, ones who know you and ones who don't."

Hope shone in Chyna's eyes. "I know things I can't tell anyone, ever," she whispered. "Two of his cousins have been in prison, and his brother boasted he knew how to dispose of a body. I know they do some pretty bad things when they're off supposedly hunting, but I have no real proof and didn't see them do anything."

All about her, Red thought. *These classes are all about her, because Barrett wants her. Those two ought to get together and quit drooling over each other, so we can get back to learning the moves.*

She shot a look of consternation over to where Timbers was standing with arms crossed.

He met her glance, seemed to read it and then moved into the center of the room. "You guys ready?"

That pulled Barrett's attention back to the class. "All right class, let's go."

For once Red was glad of the PT work. She shot Timbers a look of thanks and he gave a brief nod.

After they did PT to warm up, Barrett started the class. First, he had them put on the boxing gloves, and then he demonstrated the moves they'd be doing.

Right jab. Left jab. Right hook. Left hook. Memorize the pattern. It might save my life.

Kicks would be added later.

Most of the women were hitting the bags.

"Yeah," Red said after a few drills. She shook out her arms; her hands were beginning to feel a little numb. "Now, we're talking. He comes at me again, I'm gonna bam the side of his head. Knock his ass out."

"I know that's right," Neecy-Lynn said.

They gave each other a high-five with their gloves on.

Timbers had stepped near Red and was watching. She felt his gaze on her even when she wasn't looking at him.

Taking the pads, the men pretending to be bad guys wore; Barrett had them line up in pairs and showed them what to do next. The same one, two, right hook they'd done before, now without gloves, became the base of the palm to the chest in a one, two, then an elbow to the left side of the bad guy's head, followed by a knee up into the groin.

"Begin," he said, then moved about the room, watching and making corrections. He watched the other women before switching out with Tim where Red and Chyna were practicing the moves.

"Come on, Chyna. You ain't gonna break," Red pattered. "I'm gonna start calling you broken Chyna. Get mad, girl. Hey, broken Chyna," she jeered. "Let me have it."

Chyna punched with her right fist.

Red barely felt it.

She countered with a punch.

Flinching and ducking, Chyna backed away a step.

Damn, that girl is never gonna learn this. I need a better sparring partner. I got to train to be ready for Z if he comes after me. "You're the slow-mo backwards girl, and he's gonna Speedy Gonzalez pound on your ass," Red said, trying to goad the other woman into fighting.

"Again," Barrett said loud behind her. "Go again, and Chyna, try to move forward this time, not back. And you need your head to be like a turtle, down, with shoulders up to protect, instead of ducking. Notice how when you're ducking, you're off balance, and how, when you're down, your opponent is up over you. These aren't good defensive positions."

His gaze narrowed on Chyna. "You okay?"

She nodded, blinking.

"Okay." He turned back to Red. "Again," he said.

They tried again and again.

Finally, Chyna took a tiny step forward.

"That's it," Barrett called. "Do that again."

"Again," he said.

The second time, she didn't hesitate to take a step forward, and the step was bigger.

"Yes!" Barrett said. "That's it."

"I did it!"

"You did," he said, one corner of his mouth lifting.

So, she can fight. Well, all right. About time.

"Kick my ass next time," Red said grinning.

"I just might." Chyna grinned back.

"Again," Barrett said.

They went through the moves again, and this time it was Red's turn to defend against an attack. She moved in and hit with force and speed. It wasn't hard. She just pictured Z's face as she punched and drove through.

Chyna had trouble holding the pad, the way Red pounded on it, driving Chyna backwards.

"Ha. Broke ya," Red said. "He would've smashed ya by—"

"Again," Barrett said, quickly interrupted. "Chyna's turn."

Chyna looked at him in surprise. "Again," he told her.

She looked back at Red. Putting her right foot back, her hands up and ducking her head, Chyna moved. This time she did everything right.

"That's it," Barrett said. "Perfect. You've got this."

"Yes!" She turned and pumped her fist in the air. "I did it!" Her grin stretched from ear to ear.

"That's it for today," Barrett told the class. "Good job, everyone. Now that you have the form down, next time, we'll work on driving through and flanking your opponent."

Chyna turned her grin to him again, and he grinned back.

Red looked at the clock. *Those two lovebirds need to get a room, and we need to get full benefit of these classes.*

"We've got five more minutes," Red said. "We could do it right now."

Barrett didn't answer that. "Let's go over a few things and talk about what you've learned today."

The class settled down onto chairs to listen.

"We're training to move forward, why?" he asked.

"So, we can kick their ass!" Red said. She felt Timbers' gaze as she spoke.

Everyone laughed except Barrett.

Timbers laughed quietly to himself, but Red saw him.

"We'll get to that part," Barrett said.

"You always say that," Red said, huffing.

"Point one. Red, step up here with me, and we'll do a demo."

"All right. Just don't knock me on my ass," she said.

"I'm not going to do that. Just slow-motion movements to demonstrate a point."

She got up and moved toward him. He held up a hand for her to stop when she was an arm's length away. She stopped.

"Now notice if I grab for her, here." He reached to grab her and missed. "I can't. Learn to gauge distances and be aware of anyone this close. Now, one step forward," he told Red.

"Okay." She stepped up.

He reached and grabbed her arm. He was rough but not too rough. She didn't flinch but tried to pull away. He released her. "Notice at this distance, it's easy to grab her arm or anything else."

Everyone nodded.

"I want you to practice just moving around each other and take turns trying to grab the other, so you get an idea of how close is too close for safety. So, at this range, I can't grab her," he said. "Now, at this range," he moved in closer but didn't touch her, "try to hit me, using your boxing punches."

She tried, but he was too close for her fisted punches to hit him.

Frustrated, she felt Timbers watching her.

"Now, try to grab me."

She couldn't, being in so close.

"This is why when you hit. You drive in, move forward, and try to flank your opponent." He turned and faced them. "So, you're going to have to work against your initial instinct to move backward, because they might grab you. Instead, you'll move forward and in, so they can't, and once you're on their flank, your next goal is to get away." He stepped back. "Thank you, Red. That's enough for today."

Red sat down, quietly thinking and absorbing it all, while Timbers helped Barrett put the equipment away.

Her gaze followed Timbers as she watched the

muscles in his arms flex when he lifted the heavy bags to move them to the side of the room. He was muscular from head to toe but his chest, shoulders and arms moved in a way that made her temperature warm just watching him.

He's so hot he's a distraction. I don't need distractions. She turned her gaze away from him.

CHAPTER 6

TAMARA ALWAYS INVITED Red and Chyna to ride with her. She loved horses and spent every chance she could riding. She talked about having a horse of her own, someday. The women joined her on the trail rides, except for Red and Chyna. Chyna was too afraid of the horses to ride, and Red already had her arrangement with Buck and didn't need to join the other women.

Instead, she spent all her spare time kickboxing or on the firing range.

Timbers was back for another training session, and Barrett had said that for their last two weeks everyone was going to switch partners. After the first week, the women had become more used to each other, for they not only had the self-defense classes, they were together for every meal, and other activities as well.

Too damn much togetherness. That was Red's opinion. The morning rides saved her sanity with all this communal living and everybody knowing everyone else's business.

That day, Chyna had gotten herself sunburned, and at dinner, everyone expressed concern. No one had any after-sun lotion. Most of the women hadn't even brought a swimsuit. A few had bought one on their Saturday outing in town. Red had bought a new one. A black bikini she'd worn a couple times, when she'd had the pool to herself and no one would see her the tattoo over her hip. Unlike Chyna, she was careful not to get a lot of sun.

"If you want to take my truck into town to pick up some sunscreen, you can borrow it tonight," George said to Chyna. "It's gassed up and ready to go."

"Thank you, Mr. Ives, I appreciate that," she said. "I think I will. Does anyone else want to go?" She looked around the dinner table.

Red shook her head and turned her attention to something else. Emma had made pie, and the aroma was delicious.

SEVERAL DAYS LATER, Timbers prepared to leave the ranch with Barrett. They stopped by Cecelia's desk to check out.

"Red has to go in to town for an appointment and needs an escort from Brotherhood Protectors," Cecelia said. "The women are not supposed to be allowed to come and go, even to town. It was a mistake to let Chyna go by herself. We shouldn't have let any of them do that. It's not safe out there."

Barrett's hand made a fist. "Yes it was a mistake. We're lucky Chyna remembered her training and was able to fight him off and call for help."

"That's why the women are here." Cecelia said. "To escape from men like that. I disagreed with these trips to town." She shook her head. "First the shopping trip, and then going by herself. We tell them when they arrive that they can't leave the program and then be allowed to come back and then encouraged these trips. Well, I didn't. But no one was listening to me. Told me it would be fine. Well it was not fine."

"I bet they listen to you now," Timbers said in a quiet voice. "Giving mixed signals confuses everyone."

"That's what I said," Cecelia nodded at him. "After she was attacked, they've had to make the rules stricter with no exceptions. In Red's case, this is an approved trip to her appointment. Leah put in a request with Hank for one of you to accompany Red."

Timbers quietly listened to the blind woman who couldn't see Barrett's fist or tight jaw. Barrett had it bad for Chyna. Though he'd tried to hide it and be professional. He was having to pull himself together now to talk to Cecelia. Timbers had never seen Barrett act like this.

"We're happy to provide escort any time they need it," he said, giving Barrett a moment to compose himself.

None of the staff of the Three C's Ranch would forget what happened to Chyna. Nor would the Brotherhood Protectors. No one at the center had predicted that Chyna's crazy ex would show up looking for her and try to abduct her. They'd thought all the women were safe. But every one of the Brotherhood Protectors knew you needed a plan A, a plan B, and even a plan C and that trouble could come from any corner at any time.

Cecelia said, "There will be very few reasons to

leave the property from here on out until they graduate."

"Good," Barrett said. "And we'll be here when you need us."

"I've called our request in to Hank. Thought one of you would be the best choice to go in to town with Red, over a man she's never met."

"Any of us could do the job just as well, but I understand it's a better comfort level for the women here if they know us," Barrett said.

"I'll do it." Timbers kept his expression neutral. It would give him the chance to get to know Red better, beyond the couple of self-defense classes he'd helped with. The pretty redhead intrigued him. She had a chip on her shoulder and a mouth that never stopped, but a hint of vulnerability in her green eyes made him wonder about the ghosts in her past.

"Great. Thank you," Cecelia said. "The appointment is at a tattoo parlor, so it will take a few hours."

"No problem." He wouldn't ask questions. He'd gotten used to guarding celebrities out in L.A. and no longer found it odd to escort them anywhere. He wasn't surprised at Red going to a tattoo parlor, but he was curious about what she'd do there. *Was she getting a new tattoo? And if so, what kind?*

As if she'd read his mind, Cecelia volunteered the information. "She's having an old tattoo redesigned so it's not recognizable. The tattoo artist is the owner of the shop, and he's been vetted and is aware of the situation. No one is to take pictures of the art before or after, and this will be off the books. She's paying cash. Here are his rates." She reached for a paper and held it out.

Timbers took it, looked at it, and then handed it back. "Here you go, Cecelia."

"Thank you," Cecelia said as she took the paper. "Now, we have two choices. She can either keep the appointment next week, or, the artist just called to say he'd had two cancellations in a row and can fit her in this afternoon. However, with the long drive there, you'd need to leave within the hour."

"I can do that." Today, he'd brought his own wheels, because Barrett had someplace to be after class in another direction. "She ready?"

"Oh, I'm sure she will be. She's been wanting this for a long time." Cecelia smiled. "Stay here, and I'll go find her."

"Okay."

Fifteen minutes later, she came back with Red. "Emma is throwing together a quick lunch for you to eat on the way."

Emma came hurrying toward them, holding a

picnic basket. "Here you go, dears. Now, enjoy your picnic. It's not hot—there wasn't time for hot food—but this should hold you over for a while. Red, you be sure and eat something before the artist starts working on you."

"Yes, ma'am." Red nodded.

Timbers noted that Red could be quiet and respectful when she chose to. The attitude dropped some, which told him it was armor more than deep personality.

The drive started off quiet. He put their destination in his GPS, told her their ETA, and then drove in silence for a while. She made no effort at conversation, and her hand kept moving to her left hip then away again.

Tired of not making conversation, Timbers asked, "Has this artist done work on you before?"

"No, never met the guy. I showed him pictures of my tat over the internet, to make sure he could do what I need."

"Whoa. Wait," Timbers frowned. "You sent pics of your tattoo over the internet?"

"Yeah, the private one at the center. No one can see them."

His frown deepened. "There's no such thing as privacy on the internet."

"I've been told otherwise."

"It's a risk. How distinctive is your tattoo?"

"Very."

Timbers concentrated on driving and didn't look at her. He hadn't asked her what the tattoo was or where it was. He was going to see it anyway when the artist started working on it. It's not like she could keep it secret from him.

Just when he thought they were done talking about it, she cleared her throat. "It says 'Property of Z', and the Z is a bold black one."

"I can understand you wanting to cover it." He glanced at her. "Who's Z?"

"My ex. Z short for Z-bear."

"Huh. Not his real name, I'm guessing."

"Right. That's the name he goes by in his MC."

~

RED DIDN'T KNOW why she felt like telling Timbers. But for some weird reason, she did. She watched him for reactions, but he didn't seem to be having any. Other than interested listening.

I might as well tell him the whole story. He's in charge of protecting me. And what if Z shows up at the tattoo parlor? Yeah, I'd better tell him everything now, for my own safety.

"When I started dating Z, I thought he was cool. Bad boy, drove a Harley, was in a motorcycle club. Sexy, like the guy in *Sons of Anarchy* or one of those guys in the movies. Women always coming on to him. But he chose me. I was waitressing in a diner in Philly. He asked me out, and I went."

"What kind of MC?" Timbers asked.

Wow, he's direct. Not like Z at all.

It was one of the things she liked about Timbers.

"Not a 'one percent' club, but a want to be one percent, if you understand that kind of thing."

"Yep. I'm a marine. Lots of marines in clubs. I've driven a Harley. Sold it before my second tour. And I've got tats. So, I get all that. Go on."

"We were dating, and he slowly sucked me into his world until things got bad, and I knew I needed to get out."

He took a deep breath and said, "How bad?"

"The night I ran, he'd decided he needed to pull me more into the club. He got me drunk, and then announced he was going to share me with his club brothers. Make me part of the club. Which was bullshit, because the women who are accepted as 'ole ladies' are treated with more respect than that, and aren't shared around. Basically, he'd decided I was his whore, and he was gonna let his brothers gang-bang me."

"I'm glad you got out." Timbers tone was deep and serious. His fingers tightened on the steering wheel.

She could feel his tension clear to her bones. "Me, too. I escaped a night of hell."

"How did you escape?"

"Z sent the first guy in. They'd all been drinking. We all had. I was on the bed, with a whiskey sour buzz, feeling good. Z had been making out with me, and then we had sex. But the minute he was done, he was off me. Stood looking down at me and told me what he was going to do. What I was going to do. It hardly registered before he left the room and sent the first guy in. I was shocked he'd do that, but I knew I had to get away. I wasn't down for that, but I knew they'd make me do *that* anyway."

"*Rape,*" Timbers emphasized. "*That* is rape."

Timbers cut right to things. No dancing around. All right, need to call it what it is and look it head on. He's right.

"Yeah. Rape." She set her jaw for a minute, feeling the anger, then continued, "Z went out and closed the door. Then Ice comes in, and he's dropping his pants, ready to do me."

Timbers hands adjusted on the wheel, but his facial expression didn't change as he controlled his anger.

Red watched him from the corner of her eye. "I was drunk but knew I had to fight. I punched Ice in the nose. He wasn't expecting it, so I hit him square on, and then he fell on top of me, breaking the bed. He's a lot bigger than me. Z and the guys in the other room heard the bed break, and Z yelled, 'Get it Ice!' They all laughed. Then he yelled, 'Bring her out here when you're done. We don't need no bed.' They were all laughing, while I was struggling to get out from under him."

Timbers knuckles gleamed white and a muscle in his neck started to twitch.

Yeah, he's pissed.

Red knew the signs to look for.

"I got lucky, because Ice was drunk, and he'd been doing meth. He went still and had that weird meth kind of look on his face, which told me his brain was working slow and his reflexes, too. I used the angle of the broken bed to help me roll out from under him, as he'd rolled more toward the floor and less onto me. He just looked at me, not knowing what I was doing. Then I jumped up, ran to the window, opened it, and dove out."

"I'm glad you got away in time. Damn glad."

"Me, too. I hit the ground hard, dislocated my shoulder. It was muddy, and I was barefoot, but I got up and ran for my life. Knew I had to get as far away from them as possible, and that they'd come after me."

"Where did you go?"

"Not sure how many streets I ran down. I was on high adrenaline and running as hard as I could. But about the time I was running out of wind and energy, slowing down, a patrol car drove down the street. The cop saw me and pulled over."

"Good," he said.

"Officer Miller took one look at me and said if I'd get in the car he'd take me to a safe place and get me some help."

"I'm glad he saw you and stopped," he said, his voice a little raspy.

"Yeah. I must've looked pretty bad. I was wearing a white lace bra, and it had bloodstains on it. Nothing on my feet and a short skirt with no panties on underneath. And it was cold out, just starting to snow."

"He saw your bare feet and bloody bra and knew

something was wrong. Did you charge Ice with attempted rape?"

Red's jaw sawed shut. "*Nooo.* I did not. I just wanted to get away and be safe."

"I'm glad you're safe."

"Me, too."

Timbers was easy to talk to, but she was all talked out. This was the most talking she'd done about the event, since the night it had happened and she'd told Officer Miller.

She tilted her head and looked at Timbers. The men with the Protectors were all different, but there was something about him that reminded her of Officer Miller. She smiled at the memory of Officer Miller's kindness. "Officer Miller called me Red. That's how I got my nickname. I had long red hair, all the way down my back."

Timbers gave her a glance and a smile. "The new haircut and the new name suit you."

"Thanks. I think so, too. All that hair was heavy and hot in the summer."

"Sketch me an image of the MC's patch, and I'll make sure all the Protectors see it," he said. "We'll keep an eye out."

"The counselors all swore he'd never find me out here."

"Likely, they're right. But do it anyway. Planning for the worst, and then preparing for it, is what guys like us do best."

"Okay, yeah." She nodded. "I can do that. You got paper and a pen?"

"Back seat, under my backpack, there's a spiral notebook. There are pens in the glove box."

She raised her eyebrows. "Wow. You know where everything is. Most guys aren't that organized."

"Best way to find something fast is to know right where to get it. Always good to be ready."

Red started to relax even more in Timbers' company. It had been a very long time since she'd relaxed this much with anyone. It was a feeling she'd forgotten.

Timbers was all right. He was really easy to talk to. She wouldn't mind getting to know him. "Hey, why do they call you Timbers?"

"Spent the year after I graduated college as a lumberjack up in Canada."

"That makes sense. Then you went into the marines?"

"Yeah. I was already in great shape, knew how to hunt and fish. But they still had to make me into a marine."

"I like what they made you into," she said softly, a

little embarrassed that she'd said it out loud. However, the more she was around him, the more she liked him. It also didn't hurt that he was hot. Not that she was looking or anything.

He smiled. "I like you, too. I'm enjoying getting to know you better."

She smiled and bent her head to focus on drawing the image of the MC patch he'd asked for.

CHAPTER 7

AT THE TATTOO PARLOR, Timbers checked the perimeter then escorted her in. With her drawing of the MC's patch folded in his pocket, he was ready to show the guys, but as of right now, he was the only one who knew to watch for them. Despite what the counselors had told Red, there was always a chance this guy would find her.

Property of. Some guys took that kind of shit seriously. And it all boiled down to how bad Z wanted her back.

Timbers was taking no chances.

Z could put other clubs onto finding Red if he wanted her bad enough. It might be hard to tell which clubs were looking.

Before she sat down in the chair, she unfastened her pants and dropped them. Timbers drank in the sight of her standing in a loose t-shirt and black bikini panties. The tattoo was in black against her left hip.

The tattoo artist said, "This one is gonna hurt."

"Dead would hurt a whole lot worse," she said, her voice even.

Timbers could have corrected her. There were things that hurt a whole lot worse than death. Especially if Z got hold of her again and wanted to torture her, to cause pain. He sounded like the kind of guy who would.

Watching her, Timbers tried to stay professional and not get aroused by the sight of her, but the actions of dropping her pants and then bending to step out of them, leaving her in nothing but little black panties covering that round ass, and those long legs that could wrap around a man had him rock hard. He shifted and tried to get his mind on something other than sliding those panties off and sliding into her.

Hell. I'm supposed to be her protector, not be distracted by thoughts of fucking her.

He walked to the front door to keep watch and redirected his thoughts to Z and the gang, running through possible scenarios in the event any of them showed up. Seeing no sign of a threat, he removed the paper she'd drawn on. He strode to a counter, unfolded the picture and pressed it out flat. Then, using his phone, he took a picture of it.

Technology was great. He'd have this to all the guys in a matter of minutes.

An hour into the tattoo, the artist stopped and peered closely at Red. "Do you need a break?"

"No, don't stop. Keep going."

The artist reached behind him, and then handed her a cherry lollipop with a chocolate chewy center. "Here."

"What's this for?"

"Suck on it. It'll put sugar in your system. You look like you're about to pass out."

"I wasn't," she bit out, her chin rising.

The artist raised an eyebrow. "Your eyes rolled back in your head, I could see it in the mirror. That's why I stopped."

"I'm fine. Can we just get on with it?"

"Sure."

She closed her pretty green eyes, wrapped her mouth around that lollipop and the artist started again.

Badass. That's what she is. With a high tolerance for pain. Maybe she likes it. Some women did. Which type is she? The kind who toughs it out to prove herself, or the kind who gets off on it? Lots of bikers and their women are into S&M.

Timbers moved toward the front windows again, away form the sight of her sucking on that lollipop with her eyes closed and looked out. Just the normal traffic on the street, no motorcycles or cars full of men headed toward the shop.

∼

HOURS LATER, when Red looked down at the finished tattoo, the black Z was now the body of a phoenix-like creature, rising out of the ocean, its body black and rising, behind it a red and gold fire masking "Property of" in such a skillful way the original tattoo was gone.

Thank God it's gone. Gone forever.

Z had pushed her into the tattoo one night when they'd been drinking, and she'd immediately regretted it the morning after. The tattoo was way worse than her worst hangover, because it was permanent, on her skin, and she couldn't just wash it off.

Once her perfect pale skin was marred, he'd gloated over it. Talked about how she was his. At first, she'd enjoyed him claiming her, as it kept the other men from touching her without Z's permission. No one would flirt or so much as touch her arm. It was hands-off, and all the men respected him, and by association with him, her.

But then Z had started riding her hard when they had sex, and hard turned into rough. They'd stopped making love and just fucked. He became a different man, and having marked her as his, seemed to think he could do whatever he wanted with her.

I am free of Z. Finally, free.

This was the last step of freedom for her and she felt as if she could fly. The pain of the tattoo would fade just as her past would. She was rising like the phoenix, everything new.

~

ON THE WAY back to the lodge, Timbers glanced at Red sitting beside him as she laid the seat back and rested instead of watching the scenery. Her pants weren't fully closed, so there'd be no pressure on the new ink. The artist had taken several hours to finish, and she appeared to be worn out now that the car was moving and her initial excitement over the new tattoo had faded.

"We won't make it back in time for dinner,"

Timbers said. "We should stop for dinner and get some food into you."

"That sounds good."

Her tired voice made him wonder if she'd overdone it, and whether she was hurting.

"Mexican?"

"Anything."

"All right. I know a good place." He picked up his cell phone and called the office. "Timbers here. Appointment took longer than expected. We're gonna stop for a bite to eat on the way back." He listened, and then said. "Roger that. Out."

"Were you talking to Cecelia?"

"No. Our office."

"I thought it was Cecelia. She keeps tabs on where everyone is at all times. You can't so much as sneak a cookie from the kitchen without her hearing you."

"Doesn't sound as if you like that much."

"I don't, but I do like Cecelia."

"She's perfect in that job."

"Yes, she really is. She's amazing."

"So are you."

"Me?" She wrinkled her nose. "Naw."

"What you did, getting away from the gang, not every woman could've done that."

"They'd do it if they wanted to live. I don't understand the women who don't. It's like they want to be victims. Look at Chyna. She'll all, 'I can't, I can't'. Then of course she can't 'cause that's how she thinks."

"They freeze, Red. It's a reaction, not a conscious choice. Don't be too hard on Chyna and the others. If they know they freeze, it adds to their fear and makes them think they can't. But we can train them out of that reaction. The other women are working just as hard, but in different ways than you."

"I can't afford to be afraid. That's my 'can't'. If I freeze, I'm dead."

"Depending on the situation, they are, too."

Thinking that over, she looked out the window for a while, and then turned back. "I'd hate that for any of them."

"Me, too," he said, nodding, glad she was empathizing with the other women. "That's why we're training you. So you can fight and live."

"Yeah. Fight and live. That needs to be my new mantra."

"What was your old one?"

She drew a deep breath. "It was, 'I will be free of Z.' Today, I'm finally free. So, I don't need that mantra anymore. And I'm ready to celebrate."

He pulled the car into a parking spot next to Casa de Miguel, which didn't look busy.

"This is a good place?" she asked, leaning forward to look at the restaurant through the windshield.

"Yes, I've eaten here several times. Hank recommended it."

"Okay. I hope they have good margaritas."

"They do."

∽

RED DIDN'T TELL him the ranch was alcohol-free, and that they weren't to bring alcohol in. No one had really said they couldn't drink alcohol off the ranch. Maybe their rules were because of all the alcoholics that likely came through the center. But just in case there was a rule about off-site drinking, she wasn't going to mention it.

I'll just have one margarita to celebrate. Today is the first day of the rest of my life. Today, I'm finally free.

Inside, they were seated next to a waterfall on the wall, and the plants and brightly painted designs behind it were beautiful. She'd never have guessed the restaurant was so nice from the outside. Sitting here with Timbers, it almost felt like a date. Except that she wasn't dating. Not ever again. She was done with men.

The waiter came over to the table. "Good evening. What would you like to drink?"

"I'd like a margarita," she said.

The waiter glanced at Timbers. "We have pitchers, *señor*. If you're ordering one, it's a better deal."

Timbers shook his head. "None for me. I'm driving. I'll take tea, unsweetened."

"Yes, sir." The waiter turned back to Red. "One margarita. Regular or strawberry?"

"Strawberry…? I've never had a strawberry margarita. I'll have one of those."

"Very good," the waiter said.

He returned with her drink and Timbers' tea, and after they'd both ordered fajitas, and the waiter walked away again, she raised her glass for a toast. "To a new life," she said.

Timbers raised his glass and clinked it against hers. "To new beginnings."

Three margaritas later, Timbers convinced her she didn't need another, and it was time to leave. She wavered a bit on the way to the car, so he put his arm around her.

Red leaned into him, enjoying the closeness. She'd missed closeness. *This was nice.*

He helped her into the car and she leaned back on the seat again. Full belly, warm buzz, and the tattoo wasn't hurting any more. She pulled down her pants to look at it again.

Timbers glanced over at her as he eased the car out of the parking lot. "Still sore?"

"Not 'til I touched it. I'm feeling pretty good."

"Good. Leave them down if that feels better. No one can see in, and even if they could, it's dark."

Watching him, her eyes moved to his lips, and she wondered what they would feel like if he kissed her.

Oh yeah, I'll leave them down. That feels better. Thoughts of him kissing her all the way from her lips to her pussy filled her head, and she closed her eyes, enjoying the fantasy. His voice and his scent filled her senses, and the fantasy made her panties wet.

∼

TIMBERS WATCHED her sleeping and rolled her last words over in his head. *Would feel even better if you'd come over here and kiss me.* So, she wanted me to kiss her. Before she fell asleep, she'd slurred the words, and then a dreamy smile came over her face. Not long after, she snored.

He laughed to himself. *Just my luck. She asks me to kiss her while she's drunk and not likely to remember. The margaritas had brought her walls down. Now, she looks soft and approachable. Vulnerable even.*

Which meant that Timbers could do nothing but watch over her. He refocused on doing his job and drove on into the night.

CHAPTER 8

A FEW NIGHTS LATER, Red had gone to bed early after a phone call from Timbers, who was out in L.A. again. He'd taken to calling her now and then, just to check in with her and make sure she was okay. Something she rather liked. That night, he'd told her that his client in L.A. liked him and had requested him whenever there was a security detail. So, he'd be in town for a few days, and she'd see him in class when he helped out, but then he'd be called away again.

It sucked, because she liked being around him. She could be herself, and she didn't have to put him at arm's length. After the night she'd had her tattoo redone and they'd had dinner, she'd looked for him whenever he was on the ranch or if she knew he was coming out there for any reason.

They hadn't had a second date yet, though they teased each other about their first one.

"I don't know if I want to date you," he joked. "I seem to put you to sleep. And then after all that excitement, you get me in trouble."

Well, she had, because he'd gotten an earful about letting her get drunk. Turned out that was against the rules off-site of the ranch as well an they'd even re-written the rules to be more specific after that. "Look, I'm not an alcoholic," she told Leah the next day. "I was just celebrating a big occasion. Bigger to me than New Year's Eve, right? It's that kind of drinking. Once in a blue moon is not an issue, and it's not affecting me in a bad way."

"If we make allowances for a one-time event, then there will be another and another. If not you, then another woman. Think about the other women here for a change. This isn't just about you." Leah shook her head. "I'm only giving you a pass this time, because we weren't clear enough in the rules. But that won't happen again."

A couple of the women seemed mad at her, but Red didn't care. She wasn't going to see any of them after she graduated from the program anyway. What really sucked was that the Brotherhood Protectors were keeping Timbers busy, when she'd finally decided she wanted to spend time getting to know him. Hank had so much work coming in that he was working security here tonight, with Gunny and Swede and she'd seen Barrett too, before she turned in.

Red had talked to Timbers on the phone that night, and then had gone to sleep early, so she was sound asleep in bed when the sound of gunfire woke her.

Gunfire. Here. Holy shit. Z's here.

She sat straight up in bed, and then was out, reaching for her clothes, jamming her legs into her jeans.

"Everyone stay in your rooms!" Gunny shouted from the corridor outside.

"And stay away from the windows!" Barrett shouted.

Pulling her jeans up and fastening them over the gauze pad she was still wearing over her new tattoo to protect it, Red moved over to the side of the window, and then leaned just enough to look out.

No one's at the side of the house. Sounds like it's coming from out front.

She unlocked her door and opened it a crack to

peer out. Hank was at the back of the building, going door to door, knocking, and when the door opened, saying, "Stay behind me."

The women were coming out and doing as said, following.

Red didn't wait for him. Pulling on a T-shirt and slipping her feet into her sandals, she went out the door and joined the other women behind Hank.

As he reached Cecelia's door, it opened, and she came out. "What's happening?" she asked, reaching for his forearm, her hand closing around it.

He put his hand on hers. "I'm taking you to a safer room." He pulled her out of the doorway and into the hall, keeping the other women behind him. "Put your hand on my back," he said to her.

"What's happening?" Leah asked; as she looked out from the door across the hall, fear tightening her face.

"We've got a couple of fire bugs," he said.

The women gasped, all except for Red.

Bullshit. Red didn't buy that for a minute. *That was gunfire I heard, and there's no smoke.*

"It's all right. Don't panic. Everyone stay close." He peered around the doorframe. "Swede," Hank spoke into his mouthpiece. "Gunny," he spoke again. "Barrett."

Why weren't they answering him? What was happening? Red frowned. She hated not knowing what was going on. *If it's Z, I need to be ready.*

"Get everyone to the kitchen and get them down on the floor," he said to Leah.

Leah stood counting heads. "Two more." She pointed to the last two doors. "Tamara and Chyna." She knocked on one door and he knocked on another.

"Follow Leah," he told Tamara, the short brown-haired woman who answered the door.

Chyna opened her door.

"Come with me," Leah said to her. Over her shoulder, to him, she said, "That's everyone."

"Go to the kitchen and stay down on the floor, behind the island, away from the window," he said.

Leah raised an eyebrow but nodded. Cecelia stood still. Her face was white, and her eyes were wide with terror.

Shit. That's right. Cecelia's ex had tried to burn down her house. Z's not the only one to be afraid of. Any one of us might have some dangerous asshole show up ready to do real bad things.

"It's going to be okay," Leah reassured the group. She reached for Cecelia's hand. "Take my hand. This is the safest place for us. We have to stay quiet and calm. Hank will let us know when we can come out."

Hank nodded at Leah. She was in charge of the women now. He headed toward the front of the building.

The women had just reached the kitchen when the fire alarm went off.

Damn. I was wrong. There is a fire, somewhere.

Chyna started to cry, and her shoulders shook.

Red put her arm around the other woman's shoulder and squeezed. "Hey, it's gonna be all right. We're safe."

She wasn't so sure of that, but as she looked around at the other women, it seemed like she and Leah were the only ones not scared to death. Chyna did get on her nerves sometimes, but she was her sparring partner, and Red felt the need to boost her up. "We're tough, remember? And our guys have everything under control. If this building were on fire, they'd be getting us out, not telling us go to the kitchen."

Swede stepped into the kitchen to check on them. "Everybody here?" he asked.

"Yes," Leah said, as Red gave him thumbs up.

"Everybody good?"

She gave him another thumbs up, and he nodded then turned and left.

"See?" she said to Chyna. "If we needed to get out of the building, he'd have been herding us out."

She didn't know about a fire, but she did know she'd heard gunshots and shouting.

Inside the building, the fire alarms were still going, and smoke was spreading from the back of the building toward the front.

Barrett barreled into the room and hurried the women out of the kitchen and into the great room.

Gunny joined Barrett. He hollered at the women as he waved an arm. "Come on," he said. "Let's go."

The women ran after the men as they all rushed toward the front door. The gunshots had stopped, and smoke was filling the building.

Everyone ran outside, dashing down the steps, until they were away from the house. Then Red turned back to look. Fire burned in the building and across the roof. The bedrooms' outer walls on the side where the fire had been set were burning higher, nearer the roof, as the big logs burned slower. Flames licked up into the air and across the roof on that back corner of the building. There were a few dead bodies on the ground and Chyna gasped when she saw them. Clearly, she recognized them. Her gaze clung to each as though not believing what she saw. Barrett was looking after her now, so Red didn't have to play mama hen.

Nobody needed her. Which was fine. Just the way she liked it. Everyone else was busy, either doing something to try to put the fire out or comforting each other. She exhaled.

So, glad it wasn't Z.

~

THE RECONSTRUCTION after the fire was underway. One side of the back of the building was closed off with tarps while half of the bedrooms were being repaired. The women had to double up in the other rooms, but everyone was getting along well. Red spent less time in her room now that she had a roommate and more of her time outside.

Security camera's had been installed one at the guard gate.

Red watched Hank as he installed another security camera outside the main house by the doors leading to the pool. "Kind of like closing the barn doors after the horses are out, isn't it?" She turned to Timbers. "Your security company should've done this before Chyna's crazy ex and his cousins came after her. I thought we were supposed to be safe."

Overhearing her, Hank said, "I recommended this step when I did the initial consult on this site. But the board declined because they thought the ranch was remote enough." He shook his head.

"Right." Red snorted in disgust. "They just didn't want to spend the money."

"Bingo," Timbers said. "You nailed it."

"Costing them a lot more now, I'll bet," she murmured.

"Yep," Hank said. "When you hire security, it's a wise idea to take their advice."

"I'm glad you guys where here to stop them," Red said. "The attack could've gone really bad for everyone."

"I'm glad too," Hank said. "From here on out, the company wants us to monitor things, so we'll literally be keeping an eye on things."

"Wish I'd been here," Timbers said, his gaze cutting toward Red.

"You couldn't help it. You were on that job in L.A." Red said, moving closer. "Don't worry about it. We're all fine."

She'd been thinking about Timbers a lot lately. "Tell you what. You can make it up to me. I want to go on an evening trail ride, and we aren't allowed to go riding by ourselves. So, would you like to go with me?" She smiled at him. "That is, if you ride…"

He grunted. "Texas born and raised, remember? I was riding before I could read and write."

"Oh yeah, that's right. Then I'll be in good company." She stood. "Let's go talk to Buck."

"All right." Timbers stood and joined her. "I'm right behind you."

They found Buck and told him they wanted to go for a moonlit ride. He picked out two horses for them and helped them saddle the horses. "When you come back, you know what to do," he told Red.

"Yes, sir." She nodded.

"So, you know horses?" Timbers asked.

"Buck has been teaching me. I go riding every morning, and I help him with stuff."

"I see." Timbers said. "That's good. I'd heard the others talking about you not riding with them and thought maybe you weren't much into horses."

"I'm not a big joiner," she said, avoiding his knowing gaze.

They mounted up and headed down the trail.

The horses knew the way, but so did Red. Timbers was the only one who hadn't ridden this way. They reached the creek and stopped, dismounting. The horses drank from the creek while the birds were silent, sleeping.

"It's different here at night," Red said. "I like it." She looked up at the sky. "No light pollution out here."

"I like it," he said. He reached for her hand and pulled her close. "And I like you, too." Wrapping one arm around her, he bent his head and kissed her.

His lips softly brushed hers and she caught her breath. The gentle way he kissed her settled into her body and soul, letting her know she was cared for. She relaxed into the kiss, opening her mouth, their tongues touching, exploring, and giving.

When they came up for air, she said, "I think I'd like to stay somewhere out here after I leave the program. I like this great outdoors and don't think I'd be happy going back to a big city like Philadelphia. I'm gonna miss helping Buck in the morning, and then going for a ride."

"Then stay. I'm sure there are jobs nearby. Will the ranch help you find a job?"

"Oh, yeah, that's part of the exit plan in the program. Everything is all thought out. I can wait tables or tend bar. Those kind of jobs are easy to find."

"Well, I hope you find something you enjoy."

"Thanks." She sighed. "We have to head back to the stable soon."

They were both aware of the curfew. He nodded. "Any time you're ready."

By the time they'd put the horses in for the night and made it back to the main house, it was later than they'd thought.

Cecelia was in the great room, waiting up, and when Red snuck in and tried to tiptoe through the room, she spoke cleared her throat.

"There's no point tiptoeing," she said, her tone wry. "I can hear you. I hear you every time you sneak out."

"Oh. You startled me," Red said.

Every time? Is the woman kidding me? Surely not every time.

"You know, going out on the trail at night means Buck doesn't get enough sleep. He still has to get up at the same time in the morning."

"I put the horses up and made sure everything was done for the night."

"Doesn't matter. He won't sleep 'til he checks on those horses. He'll go back downstairs after you're in your room, and he'll check them over before he can go back to bed and to sleep."

"I didn't realize," Red said. "Do you know everything that goes on in this place?"

"Pretty much."

"There are a lot of people to keep up with."

"That's my job." Cecelia stood. "Now, it's late, and we all need to get some sleep. Tomorrow comes early."

"Good night." Red headed for her room.

"Good night." Cecelia followed her toward her room.

Once inside her room, Red had trouble falling asleep. She kept touching her lips and thinking of how they'd felt when Timbers kissed her. She wished he were here in her bed, with her right now.

CHAPTER 9

Red had graduated from the program and was enjoying her new job at the Give a Whistle. It was good to be working again. She was even getting used to the patrons whistling at her. She made good tips, there was a bouncer who kept the men in line, and she was able to live closer to Timbers, when he was at home with the Brotherhood Protectors.

He'd even said he might buy a place out here and asked if she wanted to go house shopping with him next week.

This was her third week working, and it was last call when Timbers and Barrett walked into the bar. She waved at them and smiled. "Hey guys, good to see you."

"Now, why can't I get a smile like that one from

you," said the guy who'd been trying to pick her up all night.

Timbers banged his hand down on the bar beside the man, just strong enough to get the man's attention, making him jump. "Because you're not her boyfriend, bro."

The drunk sat up, took his glass, and said, "Scuse me." Then he walked away.

"Timbers, you sure know how to clear a bar." Barrett laughed. "And look at that, two seats just waiting for us."

"You two, behave," Red said, with a smile. "What'll you have? It's on me."

Timbers leaned his head to the side and gave her you know better kind of look. "Now, what did I tell you, darlin', about trying to pay for me?"

"Ain't happening," she said.

"Damn straight," Barrett said. "What kind of man lets his woman pay for everything? A lazy man, that's who. And Timbers is not a lazy man."

"I'll take a draft. You know the kind I like." Timbers winked at her.

Red laughed. "Yes, I do."

"I'll have the same," Barrett said.

Red filled up two beer mugs and placed them in front of the men. "Glad you two are here," she said.

Tonight, the bouncer was out with the flu, so she was glad Timbers would be there to walk her to her car. She was about to tell him that when a man came up to the bar from the table with the largest party in the place. "Last call," he shouted. "We all want one more."

She hurried over with her notepad. Then things got busy and she was on the run until closing. Running to the ladies' room before she had to close and count the drawer, she hurried inside, did her business, and then hurried to be back out so she could close.

Pushing the door open and coming out of the ladies' room, she took one step when a hand came over her mouth and nose, closing off her air, and a familiar voice in her ear said, "Fight or bite, I'll cut you."

Ice.

Cold dread filled her belly while the chilled steel of the knife against her neck made her freeze, forgetting every move she'd learned.

The gang was here. Z has found me.

She tried to fight, but she couldn't breathe or stop Ice from dragging her out the door.

Then just before she passed out from lack of air, she was out the door and into the night, where Z and three more of his men were waiting. Ice let her breathe then, and she gasped, taking in large gulps of air.

∼

TIMBERS HAD a bad feeling even before thinking Red had taken too long in the restroom. It hadn't been that long, but that bad feeling had him getting off the bar stool and heading down the hall to the bathroom.

He stopped outside the ladies' room and knocked. "Red, you okay?"

Hearing no answer, he opened the door and looked inside. Empty.

"Barrett!" he called over his shoulder to his buddy, as he started to run.

They both ran down the hall and out the door. Timbers was tackled him from the right by two men as he ran out the door.

Barrett barreled out the door, surprising the attackers, and another man rushed him.

Timbers was on the ground, grappling with his two assailants, who were snarling at him while trying to cut him with their knives. Keeping his cool, he shifted his weight and tried to trick his enemies into thinking he was making one move when he was really making another while keeping their knives away from him.

He looked for an opening, always calculating, while they punched and shoved and lost their cool. Always methodical and rational when he fought, Timbers was good at reading his enemy and his intentions. That ability had saved his life and the lives of his men more than once.

They weren't smart enough to figure out where his gun was to grab it, and he kept angling to where they couldn't get it, which made the fight take longer than if he'd been unarmed. Not having an opening, he'd have to create one. After rolling to the right, he was able to pull his own knife and sliced the hand of one of his attackers.

The man hissed and pulled back his hand.

After creating that opening, Timbers tricked both men and was out of the wrestling tangle and on his feet before they realized what had happened.

The five men outside, wearing their colors, had been waiting for him, ready to fight, and they had Red. He hadn't needed to read their jackets to know who they were or what they wanted. He'd seen it in a flash before the tackle. Now, he glanced over at her to see if she was all right.

She was struggling, but the bigger guy had a knife to her neck, and he pulled it in closer, cutting her slightly. The pain made her stop. She stood still, gasping.

All her training hadn't prepared her to go up against five determined guys with knives, all stronger than she was.

Timbers growled in frustration.

The thin line of blood across her neck dripped as the man jerked her tighter against his body.

It was five against three, or four against two if you didn't count the gang member holding Red, and Red struggling to get free.

The bikers laughed. All held knives. It would be an all-out street brawl; that's what they wanted.

The street was as empty as the parking lot, and no one was out walking this time of night.

A couple of them were egging everyone on with beckoning motions that said, "Come at me."

The one holding Red's neck with the knife to her throat was too close to her jugular, and that made Timbers nervous.

In a knife fight, anything could go wrong, and the bastard had already cut her once.

On their side, Barrett, a former Green Beret, collected knives and even made his own. He trained constantly in knife fighting. Timbers knew Barrett would have his back.

As a Marine, Timbers had done his share of knife fighting. He suspected the motorcycle gang hadn't nearly the amount of training the two of them had.

Barrett pulled his knife to counter the gang member who already had his knife out and was advancing.

∽

Red watched in horror as Ice held the knife to her throat.

Ice had pulled her out the door and then the gang had waited for Timbers, and there was nothing she could've done to warn him.

Z would kill Timbers, and her, too. He'd stood wearing his usual jeans and black t-shirt beneath his jacket as he watched her with cold eyes when Ice pulled her through the doorway. "You knew I'd find you," he gloated. "You're mine, remember? You wear my mark so you won't ever forget."

She narrowed her eyes at him and glared. It would've been tempting to tell him that mark was now gone, but she knew better than to provoke him.

The door burst open and Timbers ran out, his gaze upon her.

She watched Timbers come out the door and wanted to scream a warning, but she couldn't, and then Razor and Peppers ambushed him. He went down beneath the tackle.

"Get him," Z shouted to his men.

∽

TIMBERS WAS ALREADY on the ground, when Barrett came out the door right behind him, and Sam rushed him.

The gang hadn't known about Barrett and weren't prepared, but they all had knives, and she knew they'd fight dirty. Down in the gutter dirty, and Z wouldn't care who they killed.

He laughed and egged the men on.

Her heart raced as she watched the men on the ground, rolling and wrestling, grappling with each other, knives in Razor's and Pepper's hands, and Timbers empty-handed, trying to fight them off. She could hardly bear to watch, but couldn't turn away.

Sam and Barrett were fighting. Sam was a newer member of the gang, and he'd only been a prospect before she'd run. He was wearing his new jacket, which meant he'd done something bad to earn his place.

That was the only way into Z's gang. Kill. Rape. Deal drugs. Rob.

She'd been so blind when she'd first met Z, but the blinders were off now.

If she'd known where the bodies were buried, she'd have turned him in, and she wouldn't be in this situation now.

Z had been the only one holding back, letting his men do the work and now Z and Ice were the only ones standing and watching. But they were just as deadly.

She could feel the cut Ice had given her, and the warm blood trickling out from it, along with the coppery scent. He sniffed at her neck, and his mouth near her ear said, "I can smell your blood." He sniffed again. "Don't bleed too much. Z says I can fuck you right after he's done."

That meant Ice had moved into second place and was now Z's right-hand man. Viper wasn't here tonight, which meant he must be dead. That was the only way a man left this gang.

The words Ice had spoken and the sight before her nearly made her close her eyes, but she couldn't, wouldn't, block it out. She had to stay present and wait for the right moment to fight. She had to be strong.

Everything was happening so fast, and she didn't know where to look as knives flashed under the streetlights and men fought to kill or be killed.

She watched Razor and Barrett squaring off. Razor was the member of the gang who most loved knives and fighting with knives. He could easily kill Barrett.

Razor fiercely slashed and missed as Barrett ducked beneath Razor's swinging blade.

Barrett's swing sliced the biker's face.

∽

Timbers, trusting Barrett could handle the other two, focused on Z.

The man he assumed was Z was clearly in charge and stood back in a black T-shirt and jeans. Not a tall or a big man, he was compact, calm, and staring at Timbers, his focus drawn by the likely knowledge Timbers was somehow with the woman he considered his property.

Timbers moved in. As a trained marine, he had no fear of scum like Z. The moment Timbers was in striking distance, Z lunged with the knife, aiming for Timbers' face.

Timbers jerked his body back to avoid the thrust, just as one of the bikers ran into his shoulder and fell away.

Off-balance now, Timbers threw an adrenaline-filled right hook that hit Z in the nose, which exploded, shattering cartilage and spraying blood everywhere.

Z fell backwards, still holding the knife and blinking to see through watering eyes. Z lunged again, but in pain and disoriented, his move was slower.

Timbers grabbed his wrist and took the knife away from him as Z wavered on unsteady legs. He tossed away Z's knife.

Timbers shifted his grip on his own knife, and then slashed backward across Z's upper chest to the left.

Z was now bleeding from his nose and chest. Z lifted his hand to wipe at the blood dripping off chin. Then he dropped into a crouch, his shoulders slumping.

Peppers and Razor were now both fighting Barrett, and it looked close.

Suddenly, Z got knocked into Timbers as Peppers and Barrett fought nearby.

Stunned, Timbers grappled with Z, tripped, and fell into the street. Z landed on top of Timbers, and he felt the warm blood from his nose running onto his chest and face.

Timbers pushed Z off, hard.

Z was out of fight and collapsed onto his side. He tried to get up once but fell again.

By the time he slowly staggered to his feet, bleeding profusely, police sirens wailed and blue lights flashed at the end of the street, as two police cars headed their way.

Z tried to back away from Timbers and tripped backwards over his own knife on the ground.

"Police," an officer spoke using his loud speaker. "Put your hands up where we can see them."

Timbers glanced at Ice, holding the knife on Red.

Ice turned. Seeing there was no escape, he abandoned Red and started to run.

Red, now free, kicked at Ice's knee and connected hard.

He went down to his knees.

She jumped on his back, slamming him forward.

He hit the ground hard, slamming his head, and

then pushed up again, shaking his head as if he was dizzy.

She grabbed his arm and twisted it behind his back, pinning him to the ground, and then placing her knee on his back.

By then, police were out of their cars and running up to apprehend the gang.

Everyone had complied with the police officer's command, except for Ice, who was on the ground, and Red who was holding him.

He wasn't going anywhere.

A policeman came up to her and taking out a pair of handcuffs, and clipped them on Ice's wrists. "I've got him, miss," he said. "You can let go now."

Red let go of him and stood then turned and grinned at Timbers.

"Son of a bitch. I just took Ice down."

"Yes you did," Timbers nodded, pride shining in his eyes.

She turned back to Ice. "You're going to jail, Ice," she said. "Attempted murder. I'll file charges this time. I'm not afraid of you."

She scanned the men kneeling on the ground, glaring at each member of the gang in turn. "I'm not afraid of any of you."

Timbers couldn't keep the grin off his face. She'd

done it. "Damn, girl," he said. "You're a quick learner."

"Trained by the best," she said, smiling back at him.

The fight was over. No one had been killed. Red was safe, and she'd even taken one of the gang down. This time she agreed to press charges when she hadn't before.

The shelter still had pictures from the night she'd arrived. They always took pictures, which could later help in court cases. After this attack, it wouldn't be hard for anyone to believe what had happened to her in Philadelphia.

Timbers and Barrett exchanged glances and silent communication. They weren't joyful, though this was a victory. They'd just spent a lot of energy in the fight and were coming down from the high adrenaline rush that only people in their line of work would understand. Bravado wasn't part of what they were feeling.

What had happened today was minor compared to what occurred in war zones. No one was killed. Everyone would go home or go to jail. Still, Timbers felt relieved, because you just never knew how a knife fight would turn out.

The main thing was that Red was now safe for

good. And that she was no longer afraid of Z and his gang.

Timbers couldn't have been prouder.

The police took over the scene. It would be hours before any of them could go home and wash away the blood, the dirt, and sweat from their bodies and clothes.

CHAPTER 10

TIMBERS STOOD IN THE SHOWER, washing the blood and grime down the drain. He wanted to be clean and smelling good when he headed over to see Red. Nothing was more important than seeing her right now. He needed to reassure himself that she was good. That they were good.

He hoped they had a future. Things had been going well, heading that direction. He wanted to date her. Seriously date her. Find out how far this would go. He hoped when she put everything to do with Z into the past, that he wouldn't get lumped in there with that mess. He understood she wanted to forget everything about Z, erase it and move on.

Seeing her beneath that knife had opened him up

so wide, he'd finally admitted what she meant to him. He was attracted to her spunk, ever her mouthiness and her walls. He was attracted to the woman behind those walls.

Letting a person in to see you in your vulnerable moments wasn't an easy thing.

She'd trusted him and let him in. And he was honored that she'd let him in behind those walls to see the real her. The woman who wasn't being mouthy, always pushing everyone away.

So, he was headed to see her, first to make sure she was okay, and second to talk to her about taking it to the next level.

～

THE MINUTE TIMBERS walked through the front door, Red knew it and turned to face him. This awareness wasn't something she could've explained to anyone, but when he was near, she always knew, even before he spoke.

Red, tired of holding back, wanted nothing more than to go to him and kiss him. With every ounce of her being. She wanted to kiss him long and hard, and then fall into bed with him.

She ran up to him and put her arms around his neck.

He bent his head down and kissed her, soft at first, and then long and deep.

When they came up for air, Red, who'd learned to be bold, in her time with the club, said, "I want to go back to your place tonight, and not come back here until morning."

Timbers eyes darkened with desire. "You want to spend the night with me?"

"In your bed, naked, all night long, just you and me," she said. "If you're up for that."

The way they were pressed together; it was evident to both of them that he was more than up for that. But he spoke the words anyway with a smile, "Hell, yeah, I'm up for that. And more. Whatever you're ready for."

"Then let's go."

"All right. I came over to talk to you, wasn't exactly expecting this."

"We can talk in the car." She knew what she wanted and had an urgency now, to get it.

"Okay, after you darlin'."

She shivered. "I love it when your Texan comes out."

"Oh, you do?"

"Yeah, and all these riding lessons I've been takin' are gonna come in handy tonight."

He chuckled and held her hand as he led her into the parking lot.

They reached the car, and he opened the door for her and waited while she buckled her seatbelt.

She gave him a sly glance and noticed how hard he was beneath his jeans.

Oh yeah, she wanted some of that. No, all of that. For as long as he'd give it to her. She missed sex, and she didn't see the point in waiting. Life was too short to wait. What if she'd been killed in that street fight? No, waiting wasn't something she was willing to do any more. Not when it came to Timbers. She wanted him bad.

If it didn't last, this thing between them, well, at least she'd know what it felt like to have him inside her. To ride him until they both came. They'd see where all this hunger led.

Back at his place, she glanced around, never having been there before. She pointed. "That your bedroom?"

"Yes, and I apologize my place isn't cleaner. I didn't expect company so soon."

"I'm here to see you. All of you. Not your place," she said. "I just want to see you naked."

"Well, all right." He said. "I won't argue with that."

She took his hand and pulled. "Come on lover."

"I'm at your command," he said.

She pulled him into the bedroom, and then turned to him and reached for the bottom of his T-shirt.

He went along with her, a big grin on his face.

She pulled the shirt up his body, and when it was off, she tossed in on the floor without looking at it. Then she bent down on one knee and started to unbuckle his jeans. After pulling the zipper down, her eyes widened. "Hey, you go commando. Now, that is hot."

He chuckled. "You like that."

"Oh, hell yeah," she said.

She had his jeans past his hips now, and his cock stood ready at attention.

"I like it, and I'm going to lick it," she purred.

He spread his arms wide. "Do as you will. I'm all yours."

She gave him a lick, and then smiled up at him and wrapped her lips around his cock.

He groaned. "Oh baby, yes."

She sucked him up and down a few times, and then stopped and stood.

He arched an eyebrow and watched her, waiting.

"I need to lose these jeans. Not comfortable."

"Let me help you."

"No, I'll do it." She stepped away then eased the jeans off until she was out of them, standing in those black bikini panties he'd seen her in before.

He licked his lips; his eyes darkening, and then motioned with his finger. "Come here."

She stepped closer, and he took the finger he'd motioned with and pulled her panties down to her knees, his eyes widening at the sight of her. "Smooth and clean," he murmured.

It was on the tip of her tongue to say that was how Z had liked her, and she'd gotten into the habit of shaving everywhere. But she didn't want thoughts of Z in her head, so she'd push them away after she said this one thing. "I want you to fuck me until I forget anywhere he's ever been," she whispered.

Timbers pulled her close and kissed her hard on the lips. Then pulled back, just far enough that he could speak, but still close enough that when he spoke as his lips lightly brushed hers. "I'm going to make love to you until you forget his name. Until every inch of skin he touched forgets every memory of him. And I'm going to fuck you until you call my name."

Her eyes, already heavy-lidded from the kiss, closed as he spoke, and when he finished she whispered one word. "Yes."

"Do you want me to take over now, and take care of that for you?"

"Yes. Take over and take me. Make me forget."

This was what she needed. What she wanted.

She could ride him hard any time. She was good at hard, fast sex. She'd had less experience with this. Making love with Z had never been like this, even in the beginning. It had been a way to groom her to be what he wanted later, to make her want him. She needed good loving on her whole body to erase what remained of him. And she wanted Timbers bad.

Every part of her soul told her this time it was the real thing, this was a man who cared about her, a man who would give to her instead of taking from her.

"Yes," she repeated the words, as he took her by the hand and brought her to his bed.

He went down on one knee, unbuttoned her blouse, and slid it off her arms and down her back, until it fell onto the floor.

His hands rose to cup her breasts, and his thumbs flicked over her hard nipples.

She gasped, and her nipples hardened even further.

Then he reached around her, and with a quick flick, her bra was unfastened and sliding down her arms.

She let it fall.

He bent to take one nipple in his mouth and gently sucked.

She moaned, wanting to touch him, reached for his head and ran her fingers through his hair.

He lifted his head and walked her backward toward the bed, and she lay back upon it. He reached for one leg and, running his hands down her silky skin to her ankle, took off one shoe. Then he repeated the action with her other leg.

Now that she was completely naked, he drank in the sight of her. "Beautiful," he said.

Blushing beneath the compliment, she said, "Thank you."

Holding her ankles, he went to his knees and lowered his head, saying. "I've been wanting to taste you."

"Then taste me quick. Don't wait," she said.

His tongue flicked over her folds again and again.

Then his tongue dipped into her pussy and flicked upward until finding her clit, and then he began a rapid flicking.

Keeping this up until she was up and over the edge, coming, he was relentless with his tongue. Barely had she finished. When he was running his mouth up the inside of her leg, covering her with kisses and licks, making her skin come alive for him.

He kept up the onslaught for endless moments, making her beg, making her call his name, and only when he'd kissed nearly every inch of her, did he enter her pussy, moving his cock in and out so slowly she thought she'd die.

The small death. She'd heard it called that. She didn't know one could have a series of small deaths, one after the other.

Her body was like an instrument being played by a master, and he took her to where she not only called out his name, she forgot how to speak a name, caught up into the sensations.

Timbers gave her the best night of her life.

Years later, she would look back at that night and realize she'd never again spoken Z's name.

Timbers had rewritten her story on her skin and under her skin, inside of her and outside of her. In the process, she'd fallen in love with him. Something she'd thought she'd never do again. But everything was different now.

Now, they were together. Maybe forever, though she didn't like to think in those terms. She'd told him that when she did decide to marry, she wanted the longest engagement known to man, and there were things she wanted to do with her life first.

She wasn't trying to please a man any more, doing whatever he wanted her to do. And Timbers wouldn't have asked that of her. This relationship was not like any she'd ever had.

He'd convinced her not to go back to bartending, saying, "Nothing good ever happens in bars at two a.m."

She'd agreed with him on that one, because that had certainly been her experience. And she respected that he didn't want his woman in situations like that, which weren't safe ones.

Instead, she went back to school, starting at a local college and working toward a degree in criminal justice. The police had wanted her to tell them as much as she could about Z's M.C. and any other motorcycle clubs, and she'd even talked to the FBI to help them with a couple cases.

Little things she hadn't known were important helped law enforcement to send every single member of the gang to prison and had even solved a couple of missing person's cases. She liked the feeling of satisfaction that knowledge gave her and wanted to do more to help solve crimes and put killers behind bars.

She found herself being less sarcastic and laughing more.

It was as if Timbers had lightened her, leaving her able to laugh when he entered a room. A couple times a month, he took her to a comedy club, because he said her studies were too serious and she needed to laugh more. Every time they went she laughed her ass off, and if you were to ask her, she would have said meeting Timbers was the best thing that had ever happened to her in her life.

~

THEY WERE COMING out of the comedy club, and she was wiping her eyes, because she'd laughed so hard she'd cried. The night sky was clear as it can only be in Montana, with the stars sparkling and the air clear and crisp.

Timbers paused, looking up at the sky. "Let's not go straight home," he said. "It's a full moon tonight, and the stars are out. Let's go for a drive."

"All right," she said. "It is a perfect night to be out beneath the stars."

"I agree," he said with a smile.

They got into his truck, and he drove them out of town, out to where there were no city lights or houses. Just big expanses of land and the night sky.

He drove for a while, and they listened to a few soft country tunes with the windows down, while he whistled.

Smiling, she leaned back against her seat, feeling like there was no better place in the world to be and no better person to be with.

He turned down a dirt road and drove until he pulled it into a field and parked. "Let's get out and sit on the tailgate. We can watch the stars," he said.

"Oh, that sounds nice." She smiled at him.

He smiled back. Then he took an old Indian blanket out from behind his seat and went to the back of the truck to put the tailgate down and spread the blanket for them.

She got out of the truck, and he helped her up

into the truck bed where she sat and waited for him to join her.

Gazing up at the stars and moon, she thought it must be the most beautiful night she'd ever seen. Everything perfect. They were happy together, and this new life of hers was everything she'd always wanted.

"Penny for your thoughts," he said.

She might've said, "Oh, they're worth more than that," but she didn't. Instead, she said softly, "I'm just happy. Happier than I've ever been."

He leaned in and kissed her then, sweet and long. When he stopped, and she opened her eyes, he said, "There's just one thing that could make me happier than I am right now."

She smiled a teasing smile and said, "Getting naked in the back of your truck right now?"

"Well, that wasn't what was on my mind at this very moment, but I'm certainly up for that very soon, and it would make me very happy."

She laughed. "Oh, very, very. Then let's make you very happy." She reached for her blouse to pull it over her head

He stopped her hands. "Wait," he said.

"Wait? Well, that's a first."

"Hush." He placed a finger on her lips, silencing

her.

She smiled beneath his fingertip, waiting and feeling the touch of his finger on her lips.

"I'll kiss those lips again in a minute, but first I want to ask you something."

Waiting, she remained silent, and when he took her hand in his, she still didn't guess what he was going to do until he took his finger away from her lips, reached his hand into his pocket and said, "Phoebe Red Adams, will you marry me?"

Her jaw dropped.

Marry? He wants to marry me. Oh wow. He does.

It took a minute for what he'd said to register in her mind, and then, realizing he was still waiting, she whispered, "A long engagement?"

"As long as you want, darlin', as long as you are by my side. We'll pick the date together."

She breathed in. The 'we' he often said was something she still wasn't quite used to. The togetherness and equality in their relationship. That wouldn't change once they were married. He wasn't the controlling type. There was no one in the world she trusted more than Timbers, and she loved him very much.

"Yes," she breathed the word out. "Yes, I will marry you."

"Now, I'm the happiest I have ever been," he said.

"Me, too."

He slipped the diamond ring onto her finger where it fit perfectly. Then he kissed her.

They sat together, looking at the stars for a while, enjoying the night sky, and then she said, "About that getting naked part... Do you think you're ready now?"

In a flash, he had pulled her down onto the blanket. "Hell, yeah. I thought you'd never ask."

She giggled, and he began pulling off his clothes, which just made her giggle harder.

When he was naked, he stopped and looked at her, his expression very serious. "You know what I just realized?"

She grew still, her eyes widening as she wondered what had changed his mood so fast. "What?"

"I've never heard you giggle before." His sexy voice deepened; his eyes darkened. "I'd like to hear that more often."

"Oh, okay," she said. "But I don't giggle much. It's not really me."

"Well, if it wasn't you giggling, then who was it? You know you don't have to always be the tough girl with me. If you haven't felt happy enough to giggle, then we need to change that. Maybe, you haven't had much to giggle about before."

She shrugged. "Biker chicks have to be tough."

"What? You can't be tough and still giggle when you want to? That'd be a shame. And anyway, you decide the kind of chick you want to be. To hell with what other people think." Then he smiled.

She wondered what he was thinking.

He put his hands beneath her blouse and started to pull it up, tickling his fingers up her ribs cage, making her giggle all over again.

Soon the blouse was over her head, and her breasts were bared beneath the moon.

"Look at that," he said. "I think giggling turns you on." He bent to kiss one nipple and then the other.

She sank back on the blanket and gazed up at the stars and moon, and at him.

He eased up her skirt and slid a finger beneath her panties and into her folds. "You're so wet tonight. But you're not naked. I thought you wanted to get naked."

"I do, and I want to ride you."

"Oh, you do?"

"Yes. Trade places."

"My, my. She gets engaged and gets bossy."

She bit her lower lip. "Please, trade places."

"As you wish, my lovely bride to be." He winked.

He traded places and soon she was riding him up and down beneath the full moon, which promised new beginnings and beautiful new things.

He held out until she came, throwing back her head and shouting his name to the sky. And when they were fully sated, he held her close until she closed her eyes.

THE END

NOTE FROM THE AUTHOR

I hope and pray that one day domestic abuse will no longer take place anywhere. Until that day ... Please know that if this has happened to you, you are not alone and you are loved. Reach out to someone, anyone, and let one of us help. – Debra Parmley, founder Shimmy Mob Memphis.

United States International Domestic Abuse Hotline 1-800-799-SAFE (7233), or 1-800-787-3224 (TTY)

For more information about domestic abuse, resources and information about international Shimmy Mob go to

www.ShimmyMob.com

ORIGINAL BROTHERHOOD PROTECTORS SERIES

BY ELLE JAMES

Brotherhood Protectors Series

Montana SEAL (#1)

Bride Protector SEAL (#2)

Montana D-Force (#3)

Cowboy D-Force (#4)

Montana Ranger (#5)

Montana Dog Soldier (#6)

Montana SEAL Daddy (#7)

Montana Ranger's Wedding Vow (#8)

Montana SEAL Undercover Daddy (#9)

Cape Code SEAL Rescue (#10)

Montana SEAL Friendly Fire (#11)

Montana SEAL's Bride (#12) TBD

Montana Rescue

Hot SEAL, Salty Dog

ABOUT ELLE JAMES

ELLE JAMES also writing as MYLA JACKSON is a *New York Times* and *USA Today* Bestselling author of books including cowboys, intrigues and paranormal adventures that keep her readers on the edges of their seats. With over eighty works in a variety of sub-genres and lengths she has published with Harlequin, Samhain, Ellora's Cave, Kensington, Cleis Press, and Avon. When she's not at her computer, she's traveling, snow skiing, boating, or riding her ATV, dreaming up new stories. Learn more about Elle James at www.ellejames.com

Website | Facebook | Twitter | GoodReads | Newsletter | BookBub | Amazon

Follow Elle!
www.ellejames.com
ellejames@ellejames.com

facebook.com/ellejamesauthor

twitter.com/ElleJamesAuthor

Made in the USA
Middletown, DE
15 February 2019